OAK LAWN PUBLIC LIBRARY

3 1186 00835

P9-CQV-951

THE WITCH HUNTER CHRONICLES

THE SCOURGE OF JERICHO

THE WITCH HUNTER CHRONICLES

THE SCOURGE OF JERICHO

STUART DALY

JUN 1 3 2013

OAK LAWN LIBRARY

RANDOM HOUSE AUSTRALIA

A Random House book
Published by Random House Australia Pty Ltd
Level 3, 100 Pacific Highway, North Sydney NSW 2060
www.randomhouse.com.au

First published by Random House Australia in 2011

Copyright © Stuart Daly 2011

The moral right of the author has been asserted.

All rights reserved. No part of this book may be reproduced or transmitted by
any person or entity, including internet search engines or retailers, in any form
or by any means, electronic or mechanical, including photocopying (except under
the statutory exceptions provisions of the Australian *Copyright Act 1968*), recording,
scanning or by any information storage and retrieval system without the prior
written permission of Random House Australia.

Addresses for companies within the Random House Group can be found at
www.randomhouse.com.au/offices.

National Library of Australia
Cataloguing-in-Publication Entry

Author: Daly, Stuart
Title: The scourge of Jericho / Stuart Daly
ISBN: 978 1 74275 052 1 (pbk)
Series: Daly, Stuart. Witch hunter chronicles; 1
Target Audience: For secondary school age
Subjects: Witch hunting – Juvenile fiction
Dewey Number: A823.4

Cover illustration and design by Sammy Yuen
Maps by Stuart Daly and Anna Warren
Internal design by Midland Typesetters
Typeset in 12/16 Minion by Midland Typesetters, Australia
Printed in Australia by Griffin Press, an accredited ISO AS/NZS 14001:2004
Environmental Management System printer

In memory of my parents

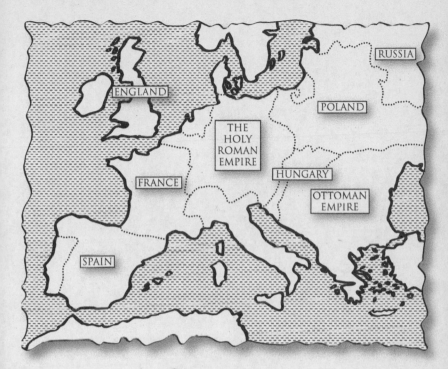

Europe in 1666

ENGLAND

DUTCH
REPUBLIC
Rotterdam
Breda
Bremen

SPANISH
NETHERLANDS

WESTPHALIA

POMERANIA

BRANDENBURG

PRUSSIA

POLAND

Harz
Mountains
Burg Grimmheim

SAXONY
Wurzen
Dresden

SILESIA

Paris

FRANCE

WÜRTTEMBERG

BOHEMIA

AUSTRIA

HUNGARY

LORRAINE

BAVARIA

Vienna

FRANCHE-
COMTÉ

SWITZERLAND

SAVOY

PIEDMONT

THE
MILANESE

PARMA

MODENA

REPUBLIC
OF
VENICE

OTTOMAN
EMPIRE

The Holy Roman Empire in 1666

CHAPTER ONE

F our riders, their collective scars a timeline of every major battle fought in the German states over the turbulent course of the past decade. All members of the Hexenjäger – an elite order of witch hunters – clad in their trademark crimson tabards and wide-brimmed hats, and decked out with enough rapiers and flintlock pistols to declare war on the world.

And then there's me: Jakob von Drachenfels, riding in the middle of the four, the latest recruit in the Hexenjäger – a tenderfoot in comparison to my four companions.

Bethlen Liprait's riding immediately behind me. His dishevelled hair, unkempt moustache and creased clothing stand in direct contrast to the other witch hunters, who wear the order's uniform with pride. But whereas maintenance of personal hygiene and physical appearance may not be high on Bethlen's agenda, there's one thing he makes an absolute priority: teasing me.

In the short period of only one week – the time that has passed since I was admitted into the order – Bethlen has made my life unbearable. His sole purpose in life seems to be to subject me to constant ridicule and hardship. My life has become an endless ordeal of being tripped over, having food knocked out of my hands, finding my sleeping quarters ransacked, and being the recipient of every practical joke imaginable. Two days ago, for instance, I found horse dung shoved inside my boots. There was no need to wonder who the culprit was: the malicious smile on Bethlen's face when he saw me cleaning my boots later that day said it all.

As much as I resent Bethlen's relentless taunting, I actually envy him for, despite all of his personal shortcomings, he is an established member of the Hexenjäger. Although I have been admitted to the order, I am but an initiate, yet to prove myself to them in combat. At only sixteen years of age, I am the youngest member in the history of this esteemed order. That should be a badge of honour to wear with pride. But as far as Bethlen is concerned, my youth and inexperience in fighting Satan's legions make me unworthy even of the time of day.

'Keep your eyes on the road ahead, whelp!' he curses. 'I didn't know they considered kindergarten a military unit these days. I didn't realise we'd lowered our standards that much.'

This is typical of my luck. We've been on our journey for over six hours, and the first time I let my focus stray – to furiously scratch at fleas, which I'm sure I've caught from Bethlen – he notices.

Reminding myself that civility is as alien to him as a comb, I take a deep breath and try to ignore his criticism. 'I'm sorry.'

Being my first mission with the Hexenjäger, I'm eager to impress, and I have to discipline myself not to take the insults personally. But now Bethlen has brought me to the attention of Christian von Frankenthal, and that's the last thing I wanted.

'Whelp!' von Frankenthal calls out, forcing me to look back to where he's riding at the rear of our group. He stabs a finger the size of a notched lance at me. I'm lucky I'm not impaled.

I've never really been afraid of much in my life, but this man – if indeed he is a *man* – terrifies me. At thirty years old, he is rippling in muscle, taller than the walls of the Papal Palace at Avignon, and has a stare so deadly it can repel a cavalry charge. In short, he's an instrument of death.

'This is no game,' he says. 'The enemies of Christ could be watching us at this very moment, waiting for some wet-nosed novice to lower their guard. Do that again and you'll taste the back of my hand!'

His voice is like rocks grinding. Or is that just my knees shaking against the saddle? I will most certainly keep my guard up. I don't relish the thought of being back-handed by one of von Frankenthal's granite-like fists.

'Give the boy some slack. We all had to start somewhere – even you, von Frankenthal.'

What? Kind words? I don't believe it. I could run over and kiss Klaus Grimmelshausen's feet. He's riding a few yards ahead of me, his raven-black hair tied back in a pony-tail. He carries one of the most elaborate rapiers I've seen, with a cross-guard in the shape of a wolf's head.

'I'd like to think this boy will last longer than the last initiate placed under your care, von Frankenthal,' Klaus continues. 'That's not the sort of reputation you want to earn.'

Last initiate! I don't like the sound of this. When I was first told that von Frankenthal had been assigned to look out for me during this mission I felt invulnerable. I thought it would be like having my own mobile fort. But what happened to the previous initiate? Visions of von Frankenthal torturing him to death over hot coals race through my mind.

'What was that last recruit's name?' Bethlen asks, smiling maliciously at me, as if the names of initiates are not even worth recalling.

'Don't remember, don't care.' Von Frankenthal doesn't sugar coat his words; he lays them thick, with a splat of mortar. 'That boy couldn't even protect a meal from a fly. Useless.'

Bethlen shoots me a look, which suggests that I won't survive long in the Hexenjäger. 'How long do you think this whelp will last?'

'No talk!'

Two simple words delivered with the finality of an axe-man's blow, spoken by Lieutenant Otto Blodklutt, the leader and oldest member of our small band. There is no finer swordsman within our order. To see him in combat is to witness a dance of death. A heavy leather-bound copy of the *Malleus Maleficarum* – the book of the witch hunter – jostles by his side in a protective calfskin case. He holds this in such reverence you'd think he had the Pope hidden in there.

Nobody tells von Frankenthal to be quiet! I'd rather be given the task of single-handedly defending the borders of the Holy Roman Empire than confront him like that. You have to pay the Lieutenant full credit. It just goes to show how much authority he has within our order.

As happy as I am to see Bethlen put in his place, I'm not foolish enough to gloat. Bethlen shoots me a disgusted look and withdraws into brooding silence. But it's von Frankenthal I'm more worried about. He's wearing a pained expression on his face. I hope he doesn't hold me responsible for Lieutenant Blodklutt's reprimand. It will be best if I keep a low profile for the remainder of the day.

Come to think of it, what is today? So much has happened in the past week I'm finding it hard to keep track of everything. I think it's Thursday. Wait. Yes, it is. Thursday the third of March, in the Year of Our Lord 1666.

This has been a year plagued by war, famine and pestilence. Europe is engulfed in a fire fuelled by winds of sectarian violence, with Catholics and Protestants engaged in constant warfare. This comes as a legacy from the Thirty Years' War, which saw the Holy Roman Empire torn apart by a war waged by the Imperial forces of Catholic Spain and the Holy Roman Emperor battling against the armies of Sweden, France, and Protestant Germany. Rivers of blood have been shed. The Inquisition stalks the land, eradicating heresy with cruel efficiency. So many heretics have been burned at the stake that the air now carries with it a sickly stench of charred flesh. It has become common practice for many people to carry a small pouch of dried rose petals around their neck to combat the stench. Outbreaks of bubonic plague have destroyed entire kingdoms. London has been gutted by the Black Death. England and the Dutch Republic are in the second year of a brutal naval campaign for control of the world's seas. It is rumoured that Louis XIV of France has set his eyes on the Spanish Netherlands. And from the east, the Muslim world encroaches on the borders of Christendom, preying on Christian vessels in the Mediterranean, and pushing deeper into the forests of Hungary on its western-most border.

Many believe that God has forsaken the world, abandoned it to the ruling vices of men: fear, cruelty, lechery, avarice and lust. Many believe that evil has planted its sin-stained seed.

1666. Containing the numbers 666. As foretold in the *Book of Revelation*, the number of the Devil.

The year of the Antichrist!

Priests are spurring their congregations into frenzies, proclaiming that the events detailed in the apocalyptic *Book of Revelation* are coming to pass. The forces of evil are emerging from the shadows, laying a carpet of blood to welcome the arrival of their Dark Prince. Rumours of warlocks, witches and demons are discussed in hushed tones throughout every tavern and coaching-inn.

Believing that 1666 would herald the arrival of the Antichrist, the Holy Roman Emperor, Leopold I, commissioned the creation of an elite order of witch hunters – the Hexenjäger – some four years ago. Their task was to hunt down Satan's servants, weakening the forces of darkness before the arrival of their Dark Prince. Whilst Papal Inquisitors cleansed the world of innocent peasants whose only crime was being illiterate, and were hence unable to read and quote the scriptures, the Hexenjäger hunted evil in its pure form, slaying *real* witches and demons. Only veteran soldiers, tried and proven in combat, were permitted to join.

Over the years the order's numbers have swelled, and what started as a clandestine unit of twelve has developed into a force of over a hundred witch hunters, recognised by their crimson attire and revered throughout all of Europe.

And I have been selected to join their ranks. Well, to say that I was *selected* is stretching the truth. I would like to tell you that I have been recruited for my fighting prowess. But the truth of the matter is not that glamorous. I'm embarrassed to admit that I hardly know how to wield a sword. I am simply fortunate that my uncle is highly regarded by Emperor Leopold. It was my uncle's signature that I forged on a fabricated letter of introduction to secure my posting into the Hexenjäger.

My father was a cavalry commander, who died in the Low Countries – comprising the Spanish Netherlands and the Dutch Republic – when I was only four years old. And my mother – God bless her soul – died of tuberculosis two years later. As my grandparents had passed away long before I was born, my sole remaining relatives were my uncle and aunt, who had adopted me, raising me as their own son.

Although I was young when my mother passed away, I still have fond memories of her. But I can't even picture my father's face. As a child, I used to ask my uncle and aunt about my father – where he was born, where and how he met my mother, and what motivated him to join a German mercenary army, fighting alongside Spain in the Low Countries. I also asked how my father had died and where he was buried. I had hoped that I could then slot these snippets of information together to form a picture

8

of the man who helped bring me into the world. But my uncle and aunt were always reluctant to reveal too much – too afraid, possibly, that such information would trigger some calling within my blood, and send me off on some fool's errand to the Low Countries in search of more clues. Knowing that I wasn't getting anything from them, I stopped questioning my uncle and aunt some time ago. But the thirst to learn more about my father, and hence myself, has always remained. Until I find these answers, I fear I will always feel incomplete, as if some fundamental part of me is missing.

Whereas my father was a soldier, my uncle is a farrier – one of the finest in the Holy Roman Empire, in fact. He's been master of the Farriers' Guild of Dresden – the Brotherhood of Farriers – for the past ten years. Assisted by his four Wardens, he is responsible for monitoring the quality of stables and the condition of horses throughout the city. He is a pillar of the community, respected and in demand for his knowledge of treating horse ailments. Only last year he was summoned by the Holy Roman Emperor to bring back to health his favourite mare. My uncle's greatest desire is for me to follow in his footsteps. Indeed, since the age of six I have done exactly that, working in his stables every day – washing, combing, feeding and watering the dozen or so horses he has owned throughout the years. He even organised for me to begin my apprenticeship as a Warden in the Brotherhood of Farriers next month. This would have been a position of great importance; I would check the condition of stables throughout Dresden, as well as ensure that farriers and shoesmiths were adequately trained and registered with the Brotherhood of Farriers.

But my uncle's dreams are not my dreams, and my heart was never truly in my work.

Much to my uncle's dismay, my father's blood courses through my veins and I inherited his unquenchable thirst for adventure. It has been my lifelong dream to join an army and lead the life of a professional soldier – to see the world and draw steel in epic battles. And in this darkest hour, with Christendom beset by the forces of evil, there is no greater cause than that followed by the Hexenjäger.

The order reminds me of the Knights Templar and the Knights Hospitaller: military orders of monks created during the Crusades, who I used to read about in my uncle's study – a quiet haven where I used to indulge in the history of medieval times. It's quite ironic that while my uncle and aunt have tried to shelter me from the truth of my father, and hoped that I would not follow in his footsteps, it was the books contained in their study, which I must have read over a dozen times, their pages full of heroic and daring exploits that ignited my desire to be a great soldier.

It pains me to have left my uncle and aunt without a word of farewell. I left a note on their bedside table, thanking them for raising me and for loving me as if I were their own child. My note explained that I had forged a letter of introduction and gone off to join the Hexenjäger. I know this would have worried them no end, but they at least deserved to know the truth. It would be inevitable that the Hexenjäger would contact my uncle to confirm my appointment into their order. The last thing I wanted was for my uncle to reply that he knew nothing of my appointment – or, even worse, to reveal that I had left against his wishes and forged the letter of introduction. To safeguard myself against the possibility of this ever happening, I had included a warning in the note I left for my uncle and aunt: should they ever attempt to get me expelled from the Hexenjäger by telling the order of my deception, I would run away and join some other military organisation. I had also assured them that, should things not work out with the Hexenjäger, I would return home of my own accord. Of course, I never truly believed I would do this, for I was determined to fulfil my destiny as a great warrior. But I at least wanted to give my uncle and aunt the peace of mind of knowing that I might one day return home.

I feel immense guilt for my actions, but I reconcile my sorrow and guilt by convincing myself that my uncle and aunt had always harboured suspicions that one day I would run away and follow the calling of my blood.

I might fail in this enterprise and fall flat on my posterior. But I'll be damned if I give up before trying my hardest. And I won't let someone like Bethlen be the reason for my failure.

What's this? There's movement up ahead. It's Armand 'why walk when you can saunter' Breteuil, a twenty-three-year-old fop from the courts of Paris. He's so vain he probably believes his portrait should be stuck up on town walls as part of a regional beautification program. But his foppish appearance is deceptive, for he's a former captain of Louis XIV's Royal Palace Cavalry and fights with dual heavy-bladed slashing cavalry sabres. That is, when he's not waving the handkerchief that seems permanently attached to his hand.

Armand's been scouting ahead for the past hour with a Scot named Robert Monro. Robert doesn't say much. Getting the odd word out of him is more difficult than turning water into wine. He wears a crimson cassock, and a long-barrelled rifle is slung over his shoulder.

Armand and Robert have come back to report that we have arrived at our destination. On the top of a nearby hill lies Schloss Kriegsberg.

☩CHAPTER☩
TWO

It was only this morning that I first heard of Schloss Kriegsberg. I had been sleeping in the Hexenjäger barracks at Burg Grimmheim in Saxony, exhausted from a day of cleaning the order's arsenal of carbines and pistols, when Christian von Frankenthal's gruff voice went off like a cannon, ordering me to attend a meeting in Grand Hexenjäger Wrangel's office, where I was to be assigned my first mission. Hardly believing my luck, I dressed quickly and assembled with my six present companions in the office, an austere room with creaking floorboards and minimal furnishings – more like a monk's cell than the office of the leader of our esteemed order.

Despite having spent his life as a professional soldier, it would be easy to mistake Grand Hexenjäger Johann

Wrangel for a man of the cloth. There's an aura of calmness about him, with his soft eyes and gentle nature.

The Grand Hexenjäger is responsible for diplomatic and administrative matters. His appointment is made by the Holy Roman Emperor, with whom he consults throughout the duration of his appointment, determining where the forces of darkness are massing, and where the Hexenjäger are needed. Immediately beneath the Grand Hexenjäger is his deputy, the Witch Finder General, who governs the order in his absence. Next in rank is the Treasurer, responsible for organising the order's estate and managing its financial affairs. Then comes the Weapons Master, a position given to a Hexenjäger with great combat experience, and who is responsible for the order's military training. Finally, three Captains – all veteran witch hunters – lead the order in the field. They are each assisted by a Lieutenant, who is essentially a Captain-in-training, and will take the role of the Captain should he fall in combat.

And here I am, stuck at the very bottom of the ladder, clad in the deep-brown tabard and cloak of an initiate. Even my wide-brimmed hat cannot be adorned with the crimson feather worn by the Hexenjäger. I will remain an initiate until I prove my martial worth to the order, at which point an induction ceremony will be performed, conducted in the barrack's chapel. It is a deeply religious ceremony, involving fasting and an evening service of prayer. An initiate must wear a white robe, symbolic of their purity of heart and soul. Only at the conclusion of the ceremony is an initiate handed the crimson tabard and cape worn by the Hexenjäger, their colour symbolic of the blood a witch hunter must be prepared to shed in the name of Christ.

I am determined to earn the respect of the order, and so I listened intently to every word spoken by Grand Hexenjäger Wrangel.

Bathed in the dim light cast by a single candle, he told us the purpose of our mission. For over two months, Captain Joachim Faust had been on a secret mission to locate one of the seven trumpets of Jericho. As told in the Bible, the trumpets were used by Joshua to destroy the Canaanite city of Jericho. Along with the Ark of the Covenant, the trumpets had then been stored within the Temple of Solomon in Jerusalem.

During the First Crusade the Knights Templar, responsible for the protection of pilgrims in the Holy Land, made the Temple Mount their headquarters and conducted excavations beneath the site. It is not known with any certainty what they discovered in the secret catacombs beneath the temple, but within just a few years they had become the most powerful and wealthy religious order in all of Christendom.

What *is* documented, however, is that Wilhelm Blonnheim, a Knight Templar who was present at the time of the excavations, returned to Württemberg with one of the ram's horn trumpets used in the destruction of Jericho.

He referred to it as the Scourge of Jericho. He provided no information on the other six trumpets, but told of how he donated the holy relic to his local church. It remained there until 1506. Then it disappeared. For over one hundred and sixty years its location remained secret.

Until *today*.

Captain Faust has tracked its location to Schloss Kriegsberg, a castle in the foothills of the Harz Mountains – deep in the heart of witch country!

Whoever acquires the trumpet will possess a weapon of immense power; a weapon that can destroy entire cities. They will, in effect, have the power of God in their hands. Understandably, we were dispatched with the utmost urgency. No time for breakfast. No time to even wipe the sleep from our eyes.

'*Deo duce, ferro comitante.*' Grand Hexenjäger Wrangel's parting words: the creed of the Hexenjäger – God as my leader, and my sword as my companion.

I'm terrified, I must confess, at the prospect of venturing into witch country. I have barely had any training in the art of fighting witches. My entire knowledge of witches, in fact, has been compiled from conversations I have overheard during the course of the past week, whilst I have been running errands and cleaning the barracks at Burg Grimmheim. But the one thing I do know is that the Hexenjäger slay *real* witches – not women accused of heresy for misquoting the scriptures, but diabolical beings who have signed an unholy pact with *Satan*. I take strength in knowing that the Hexenjäger accompanying me on this mission are veteran witch slayers – and that the sanctity of our mission will guard us like armour fashioned in Heaven's forges.

CHAPTER THREE

Lieutenant Blodklutt has been gone for over an hour now. After Armand's report, he and Robert Monro rode off into the forest to meet with Captain Faust, the final member of our team, leaving the rest of us to wait by the horses in a clearing some fifty yards or so away from the trail that leads up to the castle. Christian von Frankenthal is as restless as a caged panther. He paces back and forth, back and forth. I'm surprised he hasn't worn a hole in the ground. Only Klaus Grimmelshausen seems unperturbed. He sits on a log, his legs outstretched, his arms folded behind his head, puffing nonchalantly on a pipe: the perfect model of composure. If it wasn't for the occasional puff of smoke from his mouth I'd swear he had fallen asleep.

I've been using this time to check the weapons I've been

issued for this mission. My primary weapon is a rapier, which jostles by my side, swinging from a leather baldric. As only blessed weapons can kill witches and demons, my rapier has been consecrated by a priest and an inscription has been carved in the blade – *Caelitus mihi vices*.

Translation – My strength is from heaven.

Similar inscriptions are carved in every weapon I carry. Even every pistol and carbine ball, stored in leather pouches dangling from my belt, have been blessed with holy water. Such are the weapons of a witch hunter.

Dual flintlock pistols, half-cocked and ready to fire, are tucked into my belt, and a pre-loaded flintlock carbine is strapped across my back. Two throwing daggers are tucked into my leather top-boots. A bandolier of gunpowder completes the picture.

I'm not very proficient in the use of these weapons, but their mere presence offers me strength, making me feel as if I could take on Hell's legions single-handedly.

SPLAT!

What was that? Something hit me square in the back. It's soft and wet, like mud. But the stench!

I spin around, searching for the culprit, and spot Bethlen, wiping horse manure from his hands and sporting a grin that stretches from ear to ear.

I feel like going over and knocking him off his feet. But what would that achieve? He'd more than likely swat me aside like some troublesome fly and give me a bloodied nose for my effort. I'm desperate to earn the respect of the Hexenjäger and win my place within their ranks, and the last thing I want is Bethlen to ruin my chances with his insipid jokes. But now is not the right time to confront him. I don't want to turn him into an enemy by reciprocating his attack just before we enter Schloss Kriegsberg. We don't know what we're going to encounter in there. I'd like to think that I'll be able to count on all of my companions to guard my back. So it's best, for the moment at least, that I continue to ignore his taunts.

I lower my head in shame and start to clean my tabard. Out of the corner of my eye I see von Frankenthal walk towards Bethlen, his features red with rage.

He stops before Bethlen and stares him hard in the eye. Then his knee lashes out. *CRUNCH!* Direct hit to the stomach.

Bethlen's not grinning any more, and he teeters before falling to his knees.

Von Frankenthal walks away, satisfied. He is barely ten yards away from him before I hear a distinct *click*. Even I know that's the sound of a pistol being cocked.

He stops dead in his tracks as he sees Bethlen in his peripheral vision, fumbling at a pistol. Before my eyes have time to register what's happening, von Frankenthal dives and rolls to his right. He snatches a dagger from his boot, springs to his feet and aims the dagger at Bethlen's direction.

'Don't make me dirty my blade,' he says, with an air of indifference that shows that Bethlen's death will be of no consequence to him.

One hand clutching his stomach, the other on his pistol, Bethlen freezes.

'Lower your weapon and keep what dignity you have left,' von Frankenthal commands. 'And let there be no bad blood between us. You got what you deserved. The matter has been settled.'

Uneasy seconds pass before Bethlen lowers his pistol.

'We are done?' von Frankenthal asks, indicating he bears no grudge.

An awkward silence follows. 'We are done,' Bethlen finally says, then mumbles something incoherent under his breath, his lips set in a malicious sneer, and storms off to the far side of the clearing.

Von Frankenthal returns to his mount to check for something in one of his saddle bags, and I rush over to him, extending a hand in friendship. 'Thank you,' I say, elated that he has taken on the role of my protector.

Von Frankenthal turns and impales me with his stare. 'What? Do not mistake what just happened here as an offer of friendship. Now get away from me.'

Dumbfounded, I stand lingering in front of him. 'Then why did you stand up for me against Bethlen?'

Von Frankenthal releases an exasperated sigh. 'Look.' He points at a fleck of manure on the sleeve of his tabard.

'Don't expect me to come to your defence until you earn my respect, and I very much doubt you'll live long enough to do that.'

My heart drops. I am, when all is said and done, an initiate with only one week's experience in the Hexenjäger. As eager as I am to earn my place, I'm hardly going to be able to look out for myself if we are attacked by witches.

'But you were assigned to protect me,' I say.

Von Frankenthal takes a menacing step towards me, stabs a finger at my chest. The force of the impact knocks me to the ground.

'Don't you dare tell me what to do! I take commands from only one person here, and that's Blodklutt.' He then turns to walk away, but looks back at me. There's a sorrow in his eyes, almost as if he knows I will not survive this mission. 'Besides, there's no point in looking out for you, Gerhard. You'll be dead the second we enter the castle. The last thing I want is you getting in my way.'

Surely von Frankenthal knows by now that my name is Jakob. So why did he just call me Gerhard? And if I'm going to die the second we enter the castle, why was I brought on this mission in the first place? I feel like screaming the question at him. What good am I to anyone when it comes to fighting witches? All I've done for the past week is clean weapons and mop floors. I feel like I've been brought along on this mission solely to act as witch-fodder. I thought that when I joined the Hexenjäger I would at least be taught some basic skills in the art of killing witches. Instead, I've received no training at all, and now I'm heading off to a witch-infested castle.

I feel I know the kitchens of Burg Grimmheim better than the training hall, having spent nearly all of my free time down there, talking with Sabina, a sixteen-year-old kitchen-hand I befriended during the first day I arrived at the fortress. She is the only person I know who has faith in my ability to become a great witch hunter one day. I wish she were here right now. There is a warmth in her smile that I find comforting and, unlike the other girls I know back in Dresden, conversations with her are never awkward.

I've only got myself to blame for putting myself in this situation. I lied my way into the ranks of this order. As far as they are concerned, I have military experience. My forged letter stated that I had distinguished myself as a junior officer whilst serving under Generalissimo Montecuccoli, commander of the Holy Roman Empire's Imperial Armies. Given the service rendered by my uncle to the Holy Roman Emperor – the patron of this order – I was correct in my assumption that a letter of introduction from my uncle would have been warmly received by the Hexenjäger. But I wanted to make sure that my entry into the order would be guaranteed, and so I fabricated an impressive military background. I'm beginning to regret concocting that lie.

I watch von Frankenthal move further away and feel my throat tighten. The stress of the past week is starting to overcome me, but I'm too proud to let my companions see me break down. So I swallow my emotional pain, climb to my feet and dust myself off. This is not exactly a promising start to my life as a witch hunter.

Armand swaggers over. Don't tell me he's going to start on me now.

'Before he went off to find Captain Faust, Lieutenant Blodklutt asked me to give you some advice on how to fight witches,' he says, as if he has read my thoughts. 'Listen and learn. It may save your life. But first, a word of advice – you really shouldn't anger von Frankenthal.'

'I didn't,' I say. 'I just wanted to thank him for sticking up for me.'

'As I said, you shouldn't anger him,' Armand returns, dismissing my explanation. 'Now, you were an ensign under Montecuccoli, yes? As a junior officer, I very much doubt you drew your sword. From my experience, ensigns of your age usually stand back in the rear lines, observing and learning from more experienced commanders, safe from all but cannon-fire. Rather than wear your sword out, I imagine you would have worn out the soles of your *boots*, running back and forth across the rear lines of battlefields, delivering messages. I know it's not the most glorious of roles to play, but one can hardly expect to jump straight into the thick of battle.'

I nod, hoping that Armand won't be able to see through my lie and relieved that he has provided me with an excuse for not being proficient in the art of swordplay. 'I could have seen more combat.'

'I thought as much. I shouldn't really have to explain this to you, but your pistols and carbine will be your first means of defence against a witch. Take the witch out before it draws in close. Should you miss with your firearms, however, and be forced to engage a witch in close-quarters fighting, then you are going to have no option but to rely on your skill with a blade. Now draw your sword and show me your attack stance – en garde.'

Unbeknownst to my uncle, I had once purchased a copy of the *Scienza D'Arme*: a treatise on the art of swordplay written by the Italian fencing-master Salvator Fabris. It had taken me months to save enough money to buy the book, and when I could find the time, I would sneak into our stable loft, arm myself with a mop handle, and work my way through the manual's various chapters.

I assume a wide-legged traversing stance, trying my best to imitate the instructional sketches in the *Scienza D'Arme*. Armand circles around me, inspects my stance, flourishing his handkerchief as though he's trying to wave down a fast-moving carriage.

'No. You're too tense,' he says. 'Relax your right shoulder, and don't stand so heavily on your feet. You need to be mobile, ready to shuffle back and then dart forward the next instant. And you need to relax your wrist, but at the same time you need to tighten your grip on your sword.

The last thing you want is to have your weapon ripped from your hand during combat.'

I swallow nervously and readjust my stance.

Armand nods in approval. 'That's better. There might be hope for you yet. Now a little about the blade you are holding. It's a rapier – a thrusting blade, but with a flattened tip to allow a slashing edge. Yours has an ornate hilt and cross-guards to protect your hand. Such a sword is easy to handle. Lethal in the hand of a trained swordsman. A duellist's weapon of choice. The particular style of rapier you are armed with is a Pappenheimer, named after Count Gottfried Heinrich, Graf von Pappenheim, a famous German cavalry commander during the Thirty Years' War. It may have perhaps been wielded by a junior officer such as yourself in one of the great battles that took place in this country in the past few decades. But, most importantly, your blade has been blessed by the Church, granting it the power to slay witches.'

I consider the rapier with newfound respect, wondering how many battles it has seen – and how many lives it has taken. Rather than make me feel empowered, however, it makes me acutely aware of how inexperienced I am. 'I had no idea this blade had such a history.'

'I'm somewhat of a connoisseur of swords,' Armand says. 'And they all have a story to tell – a song to sing as they hum through the air. Some never leave their scabbards, hanging from their owners' sides as nothing more than status symbols. But a sword of this quality is meant to be drawn. Its sole purpose is to *kill* – to carve a legend steeped in blood.' He pauses, and considers me with his youthful blue eyes. 'I wonder what song this blade will sing in your hands?' He moves back a few yards, draws one of his sabres. 'Now, attack me. Strike at me. As fast as you can.'

I was hoping he wasn't going to say that. I don't think the Pappenheimer rapier is going to sing an impressive tune in my hands – it will more than likely choke on the very first note it tries to hit.

Armand notices me hesitate. 'Don't worry – you won't hurt me. Now, attack.'

Hurt him? That's the least of my concerns. I'm more worried about what he's going to do to *me*. Armand is not the sort of person I want to cross blades with – not even in practice. He may look like a perfumed fop, but he's deadlier than a viper.

I had first heard of Armand over a year ago. My uncle's stables are visited by travellers from all over Europe, and it just so happened that last year a nobleman from Paris pulled into our stables with a gelding that had an inflamed eye needing urgent attention. Whilst I had been busy sweeping out hay and refilling troughs, I heard him tell my uncle about a dashing young Captain of Louis XIV's Royal Palace Cavalry, who had only recently been banished from Paris for duelling with members of the King's Grey Musketeers. All ears, I had stopped working to eavesdrop on the conversation, my fertile mind conjuring images of the daring duellist.

Coincidentally, a Parisian nobleman moved to Dresden not two weeks after the visit paid by the first Frenchman. Seeking advice on where to buy horses, he had come to my uncle, and they quickly formed a strong friendship. Over the course of the following month, Antoine Chabot came to have dinner with us regularly, and one evening my uncle, his curiosity sparked by the tale told by the other Frenchman, asked Antoine if he had ever heard of the dashing Captain. As it turned out, Antoine had actually witnessed the Captain's duel with the King's Grey Musketeers. So it was from Antoine that I developed an understanding of the political and social situation in Paris, and of the life of the reckless Parisian duellist, Armand Breteuil.

The opera houses and ballrooms of Europe have become stages of death due to men like him. Armed with rapiers and a devil-may-care attitude, they are drawn to these playhouses like moths to lanterns, lured not by the music and acting, but by the opportunity to draw their blades – often over the slightest provocation – and fuel their own notoriety. It has reached a point that the opera houses are scene to more drawn blades than a *salle d'armes*, a fencing club.

Adored by women; feared by men. Their life and death determined by the thrust, parry and riposte of slender duelling blades. Such is the life led by these reckless bravados.

According to Antoine Chabot, Armand was one of the most famous in Paris. Being the victor of over thirty duels, his exploits – and his fall from the King's favour – were recorded regularly in the Parisian newspapers. He was expelled from the Royal Palace Cavalry for ignoring Louis XIV's latest edict against duelling. In this particular incident, he had fought six duels in one day with members of the King's own Grey Musketeers. His punishment: sixty days in the Bastille. In an act that would have won the admiration of any swaggering Gascon, he fought a duel the very day he was released, in broad daylight, outside the Louvre – again, with members of the Grey Musketeers. He was consequently expelled from Paris. It is said that the cries of the women lamenting his departure could be heard as far as Fontainebleau.

And now I have to duel Armand. I just hope I don't embarrass myself too much.

'So do you want me to ... ?'

The words are caught in my throat as Armand lunges forward with a lightning-fast thrust at my chest. Caught off-guard, I flick my blade up in a desperate gamble at defence.

Armand shakes his head, gestures at the point of his sabre poking into my belly. 'That blow would have killed you. Many fights are over before they even start.

Never underestimate the value of a fast attack at the very beginning of a duel. That's when your opponent will be their most tense. A witch will more than likely try to weave its dark magic at the beginning of an engagement. That's when you should seize the initiative and drive your blade into its chest. Kill it before it has a chance to cast its magic. The instant you draw your blade you become a conductor. Do not make your music routine and dull. Aim for the unpredictable. Orchestrate a symphony of death. Now pay attention. Don't talk. Just fight.'

I take a deep breath, muster my nerve, reassume a fighting stance, then lunge forward with a flurry of strikes and thrusts. Armand gives ground easily, focusing exclusively on defence, evaluating the quality of my footwork and thrusts. Then, having assessed my technique, he dexterously sidesteps one of my attacks, weaves forward in a blur of movement, and slaps the flat of his blade against my side.

I'm dead. Again!

Armand sheathes his blade, indicating that the lesson is over. 'You've got some speed, I'll give you that. But there's a lot of work needed in your technique. Best if you stick to those,' he points at the pistols tucked into my belt, 'when we're in the castle.'

I sheathe my blade. 'I guess I have a lot to learn.'

'We all do when it comes to swordplay. It's not something that's mastered overnight. Some of the world's greatest duellists are men in their sixties. They have devoted their entire lives to the study of fencing. And they, too, are learning new methods of attack and defence every time they draw their blades.' Armand pauses and regards me suspiciously. 'But on a different topic, I'm curious as to why Grand Hexenjäger Wrangel insisted that you should be included in this team. This mission will be no walk in the park. Even I visited the barrack's chapel this morning and sought absolution. You don't have any hidden skills you're keeping secret from the rest of us?'

I shake my head. 'No.'

Armand considers me for a moment. 'Strange, then, that you should have been brought on this mission. Why did you join the Hexenjäger? You're either very brave or very foolish to join this order. Most of the men who join are older than you and have much more experience in combat.'

'Let's just say that I have answered a call.'

'From God?'

'No. From within.'

Armand purses his lips in thought and nods. 'Then it's not my place to ask, and I won't press you any more on the matter. But I will say that we all have private goals and objectives. And it's often the completion of those goals that are the most rewarding, making us better people.'

I'm respectful of Armand's considerate approach. Though I'm also curious as to what motivated him to join the order, and I cannot help but ask.

'I've spent most of my military life fighting for France,' he says. 'But the concerns of the Bourbon Dynasty now seem insignificant when compared to the need to safeguard our world from the greater evil that threatens to engulf it. Be warned, Jakob, these are dark times. The Devil's servants are everywhere. All of a sudden, territorial boundaries and dynastic concerns seem trivial. And there is no greater cause than joining the Hexenjäger and drawing steel in the name of Christ.'

Armand pauses and clicks his tongue in thought. 'But I must also say that I've led an immoral life and made many powerful enemies in France – so many, in fact, that it's in my best interest not to step foot in that country for a few years. My past actions have brought great shame upon my family. And so I consider my time spent in the German states – that is, time spent with this military order – as a self-imposed exile and penance. Hopefully it will bring about my soul's salvation.'

Despite Armand's decadent past, it seems we have similar motives for joining the Hexenjäger. We have both been drawn to the order by the desire to defend the Holy Roman Empire against the rising forces of evil. Irrespective of Armand's sin-stained past, we share a common bond, and I find that comforting.

Feeling at ease with him, and hoping to learn more about my companions, I look over my shoulder, checking that von Frankenthal cannot overhear our conversation, and whisper, 'Do you mind if I ask you a question about him?'

'Revelation 6.8? Not at all.'

I raise an eyebrow. 'I'm sorry?'

Armand smiles. 'That's the nickname I've given von Frankenthal. I think it's most befitting, naming him after the chapter and verse of the *Book of Revelation of John*, which tells of the arrival of the fourth rider of the Apocalypse.'

'And you call him that to his *face*?'

Armand cannot help but smirk. 'Let's just say that I have to choose my moments very carefully. And I would most certainly caution you against using that name, even in jest. The last person to do so was one of our order, Jansen Kloost. You may have seen him walking around the barracks. He's a bit hard to miss, thanks to the broken nose von Frankenthal gave him.'

'Believe me, I won't be calling him that,' I say, recalling that I have indeed seen one of the Hexenjäger with a nose as bent as a dog's rear leg. 'But I don't understand why von Frankenthal has been given the charge of looking after me. I don't mean to sound critical, but is he the best man to watch over initiates? And he called me Gerhard. Who's that?'

'Never tell von Frankenthal that I told you this, but beneath his fierce exterior beats the heart of a lamb,' Armand says, his voice lowered. 'I know – he's giving you a hard time at the moment. And he'll keep that up for the next few weeks. But if you can prove your worth to him, you'll earn the respect of one of the strongest fighters in our order. And, believe me, von Frankenthal is the sort of man you want standing by your side in a fight. The trick to winning him over is to demonstrate your courage.

'It's rare for our order to take in young, raw recruits. But there are always exceptions to the norm, and we have been known to take in the sons of lords. We are, first and foremost, a military organisation. But it's prudent for any military unit to stay abreast of political affairs and not to make enemies of those in power. Although our patron, the Holy Roman Emperor, Leopold I, is the first cousin of Louis XIV, the King of France, they are great rivals. They head two of the greatest dynasties of this century: the Habsburg and Bourbon Dynasties. Both rulers wish to see their empires expand throughout Europe.'

'But the Holy Roman Empire was weakened by the ravages of the Thirty Years' War,' I say, believing France to be the stronger of the two dynasties, and calling upon the knowledge I had gathered from the books in my uncle's study. 'The Treaty of Westphalia of 1648 effectively ended the Thirty Years' War; the princes of the German states no longer owe their allegiance to Leopold.'

'Exactly.' Armand nods in a manner that suggests he is impressed by my knowledge of European history. 'Leopold is wary of his French rival cajoling the princes to join the Bourbon camp, hence eating away at the heart of the

Habsburg Holy Roman Empire. And so, in addition to the sons of lords and German princes, we have also been receptive to special requests from people who have won the respect of the Holy Roman Emperor. I believe your uncle is one of the finest farriers in the country. I've heard he even brought Leopold's prize mare back to health. It goes without saying that your admission as an initiate is primarily the Holy Roman Emperor's way of thanking your uncle for services rendered.'

I raise my eyebrows, amazed by how much Armand knows of my past. I wonder if all of the other Hexenjäger are privy to this information, or if it's just that Armand takes a personal interest in learning the background of those who join the order. But I now feel all the more guilt for my deception and forgery.

'And Gerhard was a raw recruit?' I ask, hoping to steer the conversation back to its original topic.

'He was the last initiate to enter the Hexenjäger,' Armand says, nodding. 'A lad of about seventeen years of age, placed under von Frankenthal's care. In fact, Gerhard was the first initiate to have been placed under von Frankenthal's care, and they quickly formed a strong friendship. Gerhard followed him everywhere like a loyal puppy. But von Frankenthal over-estimated young Gerhard's fighting ability. Last month von Frankenthal and Gerhard were part of a team sent to investigate rumours of a coven of witches hiding in a forest somewhere in the hills east of

Mannheim. Well, to cut a long story short, the team was ambushed. Von Frankenthal tore into their attackers ... and Gerhard followed straight after him. The lad was torn to shreds in a matter of seconds.'

Armand pauses and looks over at von Frankenthal, a genuine sadness in his eyes. 'Understandably, von Frankenthal hasn't coped well with Gerhard's death. It's evident that he blames himself for what happened, and he has a lot of pent-up anger. Gerhard was, after all, placed under his care, and they were close friends. Von Frankenthal has tried to erase the entire incident from his mind, and on the rare occasion that he does talk of Gerhard, it's with scorn. Mental scars take a long time to heal, if indeed they ever do.

'Lieutenant Blodklutt has placed you under von Frankenthal's care primarily to get him back in the saddle, so to speak. And now, I guess, von Frankenthal's afraid of becoming too attached to any new initiate. He's already lost one, and he doesn't want to go through that pain again. But there's hope for you yet. He'll never admit it, but I'm sure that von Frankenthal's true motive for hitting Bethlen was to get revenge for what he did to you.'

'Well, at least I now understand why he treats me the way he does,' I say, appreciative of the information provided by Armand.

'Be patient. He will eventually learn to accept you for who you are.'

'But time is something I fear I may not have,' I say, and lower my eyes. 'Nobody here seems to think that I'm going to survive this mission. And look what happened to Gerhard.'

Armand plants a hand on my shoulder, forcing me to look into his eyes. 'I'm not sure what role Lieutenant Blodklutt will have me play in the castle. Normally, I'm in the thick of battle. But I will do my best to keep an eye out for you. You have my word on that. And my word is something I do not give lightly.'

I feel my heart fill with hope. For the first time this week, I actually have something to feel good about. Within the hour I may be fighting witches inside Schloss Kriegsberg, but I now have a valuable ally within the Hexenjäger – a skilled swordsman with plenty of combat experience.

Armand comes from a world rife with gossip and backstabbing. The more I talk to him, however, the more I am beginning to respect him. Despite his immoral past, he seems to be sincere. It looks as though I might be making my first friend within the ranks of the Hexenjäger.

I am about to thank Armand, when Lieutenant Blodklutt and Robert Monro return with Captain Faust – a veteran Hexenjäger with features as hard as weathered stone. He's of medium height but as wide as a Spanish galleon, and lines as deep as dry river beds are etched in his forehead.

After a quick introduction – which, I must confess, I find anti-climactic, as he pays me scant interest – he beckons us close.

'I have important news,' he announces, getting straight to business. 'As you already know, I have traced the location of one of Joshua's trumpets to Schloss Kriegsberg. From the inhabitants of a nearby village I have learned of a local legend. It tells of a mad countess, Countess Gretchen Kraus – a powerful witch by many accounts, who acquired the trumpet we seek well over a hundred years ago. She tried using the trumpet for her own evil designs, but it burned her hands like hot coals. Having vowed that the weapon would never be used against the forces of darkness, she tried to destroy it. A blacksmith's hammer – even fire and acid – proved ineffective. So she hid the trumpet within a trap-riddled dungeon beneath the central keep of Schloss Kriegsberg. All manner of horrors guard the artefact.' Captain Faust pauses for dramatic effect. 'Some even say that one of Hell's lieutenants waits in the darkness, in silent vigil for eternity.'

Dramatic effect achieved! Did someone just pour ice down my spine? It's too late to walk away now, though. I'm in this up to my ears.

'Now getting through the dungeon and securing the trumpet is not going to be easy, but it gets worse,' Captain Faust continues, his bill of fare not complete. 'I have learned that a coven of witches resides in the castle. It is also said that the Countess still lives. She maintains her youth by bathing in the blood of young maidens. She's known by the locals as the Blood Countess.'

I feel my stomach tighten in fright. Hell's lieutenant, a coven of witches and a countess who has found the secret to eternal youth! Am I the only one to have noticed that there are only eight of us? *Eight!* We are not the Lord's angels, but mortal flesh and blood. I fear we'll be cut to shreds the second we enter the castle.

'So what do we do now?' Bethlen asks.

I know what I feel like doing – riding back to Burg Grimmheim and informing Grand Hexenjäger Wrangel that the situation is hopeless. Even better, we could tell him that we couldn't find the trumpet. It was all part of an elaborate hoax. Joke on us. Schloss Kriegsberg was all but dust and cobwebs.

'I didn't join this order to sit and watch dust gather on some castle,' Christian von Frankenthal says, his voice a rumbling avalanche. 'We are the Hexenjäger. We know the location of the trumpet. What's more, just hearing that one of Hell's lieutenants waits in the dungeon is reason enough for us to go in – right now.'

Speak for yourself, von Frankenthal! It's reason enough to make me sprint twenty leagues in the opposite direction, thank you very much. I'll gladly accompany the team up to the castle, but that's far enough for me. There's no glory to be had in rushing to a certain death. Caution before bravado, I always say.

'As much as I want to find the Scourge of Jericho, it's too late for us to venture into the castle today,' Captain Faust explains, much to my relief. 'It's already past midday – we only have another five hours of daylight remaining. Satan's followers are at their most powerful in the dead hours of night. The last thing we want is to get caught in the castle come nightfall and give any would-be attackers an unnecessary advantage. I very much doubt even we would survive such an encounter. It will be prudent for us to wait until tomorrow before venturing into the castle. If we set off at first light, we can have the entire day to search for the relic.'

'And what do we do until then?' Armand asks. 'I'm not keen to spend the night in this forest, left to the mercy of packs of wolves and whatever other horrors stalk these lands.'

'Is it the wolves that scare you?' Bethlen snickers. 'Or the thought of not sleeping in a bed, Frenchman?'

'May I suggest you leave attempts at humour to those who have the mental capacity to make jokes,' Armand says curtly. 'Otherwise, you may strain your brain.'

Glad to see Bethlen put in his place again, I cannot help but smile, but Captain Faust is not impressed, giving both Bethlen and Armand a glare that immediately silences any further bickering.

'We will camp here for the evening,' Captain Faust says finally, inspecting the clearing. 'It seems a good enough spot. We can leave at first dawn and be up at the castle within a matter of minutes.'

'Well, what are you waiting for – an invitation? You heard the Captain – let's set camp,' Lieutenant Blodklutt orders, clapping his hands to get us moving.

Within half an hour, bed rolls are laid, the horses are unsaddled and fed, and a fire is lit. We then spend the remainder of the afternoon checking our weapons and girding ourselves for the impossible task that lies ahead.

CHAPTER FOUR

Having checked my weapons over a dozen times, I wander off to the edge of the clearing to where there is a break in the trees, and stare up at the battlements of the castle, perched atop a hill that rises above the surrounding foothills of the Harz Mountains. For some strange reason, however, I find my eyes drawn past the castle, to the mist-shrouded peak of a distant towering mountain. Just looking at it sends a shiver down my spine, as if the mountain itself is emanating an aura of evil.

Looking back at Schloss Kriegsberg, I am reminded that tomorrow will be my baptism of fire. My knowledge of fighting is based on heroic tales read in books. Even my knowledge of swordplay has come from the instructional sketches in the *Scienza D'Arme*. But tomorrow I will face the stark reality of combat. I have dreamed of this moment my entire life – the moment I will draw my blade and leap into battle, carving a reputation as a skilled warrior. But now, on the very eve of achieving my life-long dream, I find myself uttering a silent prayer – a prayer that I will not panic at the first sight of spilt blood.

A cough draws me from my thoughts, and I'm surprised to find Klaus sitting on a log several yards over to my left, puffing away on his pipe. Encouraged by the favourable outcome of my earlier discussion with Armand, I decide to initiate a conversation with him.

'What's the name of that mountain?' I ask, gesturing at the distant peak.

'Why?'

'I don't know. It just makes me uneasy.'

Klaus tilts back his wide-brimmed hat to get a closer look. 'It's called Brocken Mountain. The highest in this region. But it's more famous as a haunt for witches.'

I look again at the mountain, its snow-covered peak shrouded in mist, hiding unknown horrors. I feel the skin on the back of my neck start to crawl.

'Last year the Church sent a company of witch hunters up that mountain to destroy a coven of witches,' Klaus continues. 'Not members of our order, but they were nasty fellows, nonetheless, having conducted a reign of terror down in Bavaria, and led by Heinrich von Dornheim, the son of the Witch Bishop of Bamberg. Not the sort of people you'd want to run into. Well, actually, you never will, because they were never seen again. It's as if the mountains swallowed them up.'

My ears prick up like soldiers snapping to attention. 'How many witch hunters?'

'Thirty.'

'Thirty!' I exclaim, wondering how so many could simply disappear.

'These mountains are ancient,' Klaus explains, reading the alarmed look on my face. 'They hold many dark secrets. You'd best keep your wits about you. And consider yourself lucky that it isn't the night before May Day.'

'Why? What's to be feared about the final night of April?' I ask, wondering why he would warn me about a festival celebrating the end of winter.

Klaus arches an eyebrow. 'You really don't know much, do you? On May Day's eve – or Walpurgis Night – these mountains come alive with witches as they celebrate a Sabbath. Infants are stolen from nearby villages and sacrificed in Satan's name, and witches climb to the Hexentanzplatz – the Witches' Dance Floor – a plateau high in the mountains, from where they take to the night sky on their broomsticks.' He snorts derisively. 'The Church has known about this for centuries. But what has it done? Nothing. It's more concerned with burning people with conspicuous birthmarks.'

Hearing him say this, I tilt my head in curiosity,

surprised that one of the Hexenjäger would make such an open criticism of the Church. I place a hand on the hilt of my rapier for reassurance, and look again at Brocken Mountain. Somewhere up there lie the bodies of thirty dead witch hunters. That hardly inspires confidence in the success of our mission.

'What's it like to fight a witch? I mean, a *proper* witch?' I ask, turning my attention back to Klaus. 'You're a veteran witch hunter. You must have killed dozens.'

'You don't join the Hexenjäger to shear sheep,' Klaus says, suppressing a grin. 'Let's just say I've well and truly earned my position within this order. Fighting witches is always a nasty affair. They never go down without a fight. And a word of advice – never give one the opportunity to gain the offensive. You must always press the attack. Don't give it the chance to weave its dark magic. Hesitate, and you'll most certainly end up dead.'

I nod appreciatively. Right now, any advice is invaluable if I have any hope of surviving the mission ahead.

'Show them no mercy,' Klaus continues. 'To do otherwise will cost you your own life. Under no circumstances should you allow one to surrender. And if the opportunity should ever arise during combat, take out the hag's tongue. Do that, and it can't weave its magic.'

I shoot Klaus a horrified look. Visions of me sitting on a wrinkled old crone, severing her tongue with my dagger, flash through my mind.

'Never do that,' Klaus warns, reading the expression on my face. 'Never take pity on them. To do so will cost you your own life. Remember that witches have abandoned God. And do not confuse the witches we fight with the innocent old women burned at the stake by the Roman Catholic Church. For we fight *real* witches who have made an unholy pact with Satan and gained diabolical powers. They can only be killed with holy weapons, and cast spells that will sap the blood from your veins.' His eyes suddenly narrow into malicious slits, revealing that there is a deeper, darker side beneath his calm exterior. 'I've walked the earth for thirty-two years now, and for twelve of those I have been God's avenging angel. All who stray from His true path will face my judgement. They will answer for their blasphemous actions on the end of my blade. Vengeance shall be mine.' He then catches himself and smiles dismissively. 'But that's why we've all joined the Hexenjäger, isn't it?'

Although taken aback by the sudden aggression in his words, and believing that there may have perhaps been a deeper meaning behind his threat, I am nonetheless thankful for his advice. I'm about to pick his mind for more information on fighting Satan's legions, but Armand announces that he has prepared an early dinner and calls us over to sit by the fire.

The sun has set by the time we finish our meal of bread and salted pork. As Robert takes first watch, the rest of us huddle around the fire. At length, the Hexenjäger start to discuss past missions, and tell dark tales of witches and warlocks, many of which concern horrific events that have taken place in these very mountains. At first, I listen intently, hoping to learn all that I can. But it isn't long before I draw my cloak tight around my neck, and glance warily over my shoulder into the darkness beyond the perimeter of light cast by our camp fire, fearful of what horrors might be lurking in the night, and conscious of the peril I have placed myself in.

The Hexenjäger tell dozens of tales, some of which would chill the blood of veteran Papal Inquisitors, let alone an inexperienced initiate. But there's one tale told by Captain Faust that leaves me terrified. According to a local legend, a witch, masquerading as a midwife, abducted and ate three infants in Goslar, a town located not far from our present location. She eventually came to the attention of the authorities, who followed her to her cottage deep in the forest. A fight ensued, but the witch escaped before she could be caught. However, it was what the authorities discovered inside the cottage that truly terrified them. Stored on shelves, lining the walls of every room, were hundreds of bottles containing the still-beating hearts of infants the witch had slain and eaten. Satanic verses, scrawled in blood on the bottles, kept the hearts beating – and it was this dark magic, the authorities reckoned, that had kept the witch alive for several hundred years. The authorities smashed the bottles and burned the cottage to the ground. The witch was never seen again, but it is said she still prowls these forests and mountains at night time, looking for a fresh heart to start her collection anew. It is also said that the haunting sound of wailing infants can be heard at the site where the witch's cottage once stood.

It is almost midnight before the Hexenjäger finish talking and curl up beside the fire. With Lieutenant Blodklutt replacing Robert on watch, I lay down on my bed roll, but I very much doubt I will get any sleep. The fact that we are camping in the foothills of the witch-infested Harz Mountains – and the haunting tales I have heard – have scared me to no end. If I wasn't in the presence of a unit of highly trained witch slayers, I'd be getting on my horse and riding out of here this very instant.

I have barely laid down, however, before Bethlen, lying only a yard or two off to my right, hisses to get my attention. 'I hope you get a good night's sleep, whelp,' he whispers. 'For it's going to be the last you'll ever get. You'll be *dead* by this time tomorrow.'

Trying to ignore his comment, I pull one of the pistols from my belt and clutch it tight against my chest. Facing the fire, my back turned towards the night, I lay awake for some time, too afraid to close my eyes, listening to the distant howls of wolves, my mind conjuring images of withered old crones emerging from Schloss Kriegsberg and sneaking down to our campsite, where they leer at us from behind the curtain of the night.

I cannot help but notice that Captain Faust remains sitting by the fire the entire night, wrapped in the folds of his crimson cloak, his sheathed rapier propped by his side. Taking some comfort from the fact that he and Lieutenant Blodklutt are maintaining a careful vigil over the camp, I eventually drift off into a troubled sleep.

CHAPTER FIVE

I am woken an hour before dawn by Captain Faust. I wake surprisingly refreshed, and relieved that we were not attacked during the night. My companions have already risen, strapped on their baldrics, and are eating a quick breakfast. I join them, and it isn't long before Captain Faust orders us to assemble at the trail that leads up to the castle.

'It will be dawn soon,' he says. 'We will head up to Schloss Kriegsberg now. We won't be going in straight away, though. First, we need to assess the situation and work out the best way to sneak into the castle without being spotted. We also need to wait for the sun to rise. Once it's daylight, the witches will be their weakest. As we don't know exactly what we are going to encounter in there, you'll need to be on your guard. A simple mistake could be fatal, costing us all our lives.'

No sooner has he said this than von Frankenthal shoots me a stern look, as if I am destined to fail on this mission, and that it will be my inexperience that will place everybody in danger. 'Then let's get this over and done with,' he growls, looking back at Captain Faust. 'We've waited long enough. It's time for my blade to quench its thirst for witches' blood.'

If von Frankenthal wanted to impress Captain Faust, he certainly achieved his aim. The Captain's eyes flash with an inner fire. His furnace of war has been stoked. He draws his blade, and the others do likewise in a symbolic union – a brotherhood of war. I draw mine with the enthusiasm of someone who's been ordered to unblock a city sewer with an already broken mop.

Captain Faust kisses his blade. '*Audaces fortuna iuvat.*'

Fortune favours the brave. Well, not always. And it certainly doesn't pay for your funeral service. Nor reconcile grieving family.

Armand looks across at me and winks encouragingly, as if everything is going to be all right. I swallow back the rising knot of fear in my throat and try to take strength from Armand's reassuring presence.

But then Bethlen pushes up beside me and sticks his face inches from mine. 'This is going to be your baptism by fire, whelp. You're a lamb about to be sent to the slaughter.'

Schloss Kriegsberg is enormous, defended by a forty-foot-high crenellated wall, and riddled with battlements, towers and parapets. The entrance is guarded by an imposing barbican, its heavy portcullis raised. As the top of the hill on which the castle stands is comprised of solid rock, the entire fortress is surrounded by a fifty-yard perimeter of cleared ground, making a surprise assault impossible.

Before the advent of gunpowder, Schloss Kriegsberg would have been impregnable. But stone walls are little defence against the destructive power of cannons. Now the castle is nothing more than a relic of the age of chivalry and jousting knights. Still, I must confess, it certainly impresses.

We are concealed within a clump of trees on the edge of the cleared perimeter, facing the barbican and outer gatehouse. Crouched on my knees, peering through the branches, I have a perfect view of the castle, and I can't help but shiver in nervous anticipation. Somewhere beneath the fastness lies the Trumpet of Jericho, guarded by the Blood Countess and her minions.

'Our first objective is to secure the gatehouse,' Captain Faust whispers, drawing everyone's attention. 'I want a complete sweep of the area. Don't leave any nook or cranny unchecked. I don't want anything to surprise us from behind. We'll go in two groups. I'll lead the first; Blodklutt brings up the second. Christian, Klaus, Armand and Robert are with me. Bethlen and Jakob are with Blodklutt.

The second group doesn't move until it sees my signal. We don't know what we're going to encounter in there. I certainly don't want us falling into any trap. If we do, it's up to the second team to launch their own surprise and help us out. The entire barbican is to be cleared before we proceed into the castle proper. From what I can see from here, it looks as if there will be a second gatehouse at the rear of the barbican. We'll meet at that second gate.'

Fate must have me blacklisted. This has to be some sort of sick joke. Why have I been stuck with Bethlen? I look at his direction, and catching my eye he sneers back at me. I was sure I was going to be assigned to the same group as von Frankenthal. It's going to be impossible for him to look after me if I'm back with Bethlen and Lieutenant Blodklutt. Again, I find myself wondering why I was ever placed under his care. And Armand – the one person I feel I can truly trust and depend upon – is also in the first group.

Still, if anyone is going to encounter witches, it's going to be Captain Faust's group, being the first to enter the castle. Therefore it only makes perfect sense that I an absolute novice – should be assigned to the rear group.

And it's not as if the group to which I've been assigned won't be able to look after itself. Lieutenant Blodklutt's reputedly the best swordsman within the entire order. But, I remind myself ominously, there's only so much that one man can do, irrespective of how talented a fighter they are, against a coven of witches and one of Hell's lieutenants.

A final check of our weapons, a few encouraging smiles, and then we crouch like stalking panthers in the undergrowth, awaiting Captain Faust's command to spring into action. This is all happening so fast it feels surreal. My head is in a spin. I feel a world apart from my uncle's stables, and I find myself wishing desperately to be back there right now. But it wasn't as if anyone twisted my arm behind my back and forced me to join the Hexenjäger. It was all my own doing. I just never thought I was going to be this nervous.

From the corner of my eye I catch von Frankenthal staring at me. He comes over and crouches by my side.

'Keep your head down in there, you hear me,' he says. 'Leave the fighting to the more experienced men. The last thing I want is to have to drag your bloodied corpse out of there. So stay by Lieutenant Blodklutt and watch your back.'

He moves off before I get a chance to respond, leaving me staring after him. He goes back to his original position, glaring at the castle as he girds himself for combat. I think that was von Frankenthal's way of telling me that he actually does care about me and is concerned for my safety. He obviously still has a long way to go before he becomes reconciled to Gerhard's death. As Armand said, mental scars take a long time to heal. But I'm sure that, with time, von Frankenthal will start to accept me for who I am, and not as the ghost of his lost friend. I just hope that we survive this mission and get the opportunity to develop that friendship.

Armand shuffles over to my side. 'How are you feeling?'

'I don't think I've ever been so nervous,' I say, finding it hard to meet his eyes.

'I felt exactly the same during my first fight with witches. It's a little bit different to the strategic deployment of troops on a battlefield, isn't it? There will be no watching the fight from the rear lines here. But you must remember that we are about to draw our swords in the name of Christ, and there can be no greater cause than that. Rest assured, God watches over us today.' He tousles my hair, as if I were his kid brother. 'But do as von Frankenthal said: keep your head down, and stay by the Lieutenant. And if anything gets past Blodklutt and comes after you, use your pistols. You've got two free attacks at whatever comes near you. If a witch does get in close, remember what I told you about seizing the advantage and striking it down before it has a chance to cast a spell. Whatever you do, don't hesitate.'

I attempt a weak smile. 'I'll do my best.'

I wish there was some way I could go back in time and erase those lies from my letter of introduction. Armand has offered a hand in true friendship, and all I've done is deceive him. I'm afraid, however, that if the truth is ever known it will mean my immediate expulsion from the order. But, more importantly, that lie has now placed me in great peril.

Perhaps I could . . .

'*Now.*'

What? So soon! I didn't even have time to finish that last thought. I'm surprised I could even hear Captain Faust's command over the sound of my beating heart.

Armand pats me on the shoulder. 'Godspeed.'

The next instant, he springs from his concealment and – along with Captain Faust, von Frankenthal, Klaus and Robert – races towards the castle as if the Devil were at his heels.

The five Hexenjäger sprint across the expanse of open ground and reach the outer gatehouse. It's not surprising that Armand is the first to reach the castle. It wouldn't surprise me if he has essence of lightning in his veins. Conversely, Christian von Frankenthal brings up the rear, moving with the speed of a lame draught horse. Gravel and lime mortar – that's what you'd find in his veins.

Blades drawn, pistols at the ready, the Hexenjäger melt into the shadows beneath the raised portcullis. They then hold their position, waiting to see if they have been noticed.

Anxious seconds take an eternity to pass.

I scan the gatehouse for movement, my eyes prying deep into the shadows. But Schloss Kriegsberg is as still as a corpse. It's as though the world is frozen in silent expectation, waiting for us to be lured into Hell's maw.

This is painful. The anticipation is excruciating.

But then I see movement – in the shadows, over to the left of the portcullis. I tense, and my heart skips a beat. A *witch!*

No, wait. False alarm. It's only Captain Faust. I didn't even notice him creep forward. He's as stealthy as a thief's shadow. You wouldn't want to run into him in a dark alley. He'd have a knife to your throat even before you knew he was there.

A snap of his hands issues silent orders to the others. They divide into two groups: Captain Faust and Armand move through a doorway in the eastern tower; Klaus, Robert and von Frankenthal take the door in the western tower.

I take a deep breath and try to calm my nerves. It will be my turn any minute now.

CHAPTER SIX

Time has been shackled with a ball and chain. Agonising seconds have dragged into minutes, and still there's been no sign of Captain Faust's signal.

Perhaps something has gone wrong. What if Captain Faust's team has been ambushed? Surely I would have heard sounds of combat if that were the case.

I turn and look at Lieutenant Blodklutt for reassurance. His steel-grey eyes are locked on Schloss Kriegsberg. He reminds me of a hunting dog, eagerly awaiting its master's command to tear into its prey. But I can't read any alarm on his features. I'll take that as a good sign. Still, this waiting is as painful as thumbscrews.

More minutes drag by. I wipe a sleeve across my forehead, readjust the grip on my rapier. Finally, I catch movement in a window in the eastern gate tower. It's Captain Faust, waving his hat.

The signal! At long last.

'Let's go.'

A simple command from Lieutenant Blodklutt, and the next instant I'm sprinting towards the gatehouse, Bethlen racing by my side.

'Like a lamb to the slaughter,' he taunts.

Ignoring him, I keep pace with Lieutenant Blodklutt and charge across to the castle's entrance. The carbine slung over my shoulder jostles about like an awkward appendage. It's essentially a cavalry weapon, much lighter than a musket, but I've never tried running with one before. And I don't think I will ever again, particularly when I'm already carrying two pistols and a rapier. Even over this short distance it feels like an anchor. As tempting as it is to toss it aside, I dare not abandon it. There's no telling what we will face in Schloss Kriegsberg. It's best if I don't discard any of my weapons just yet.

I reach the right gate tower. Knowing that Captain Faust has already come through here is reassuring. Surely he would have triggered any surprise attack. But I'm not taking any chances, particularly when I read the inscription above the portcullis ... scrawled in what appears to be *dried blood*.

Lasciate ogne speranza, voi ch'intrate.

Translation – Abandon all hope, ye who enter here.

Straight from Dante's *Divine Comedy*: the inscription on the gates of Hell!

The hairs on my body rising in fright, I brace my back against the wall and arm myself with my rapier and a pistol. I try to squeeze into the shadows, my eyes darting left and right, surveying every possible hiding spot in the courtyard beyond the raised portcullis.

Nothing there. Well, at least, nothing that I can see.

Good. Now check the eastern gate tower. Careful, though. I can't be too hasty. Caution must govern my every step.

I inch forward, move beneath the portcullis, and open the gate tower door. With the exception of Captain Faust and Armand, I'm sure this door has not been opened in centuries, and the air inside has remained undisturbed until this very day, brewing into a lethal cocktail, just waiting to assail our nostrils. I step back, take a breath of fresh air, and then peer past the door. There's nothing in here but a flight of stairs, winding up into the darkness. All is silent – deathly silent. There's no sign of Captain Faust and Armand, either. They must be exploring the upper levels of the tower.

A click of Lieutenant Blodklutt's fingers draws my attention to the courtyard. A series of silent gestures indicates that Bethlen and I are to skirt around the eastern perimeter. The Lieutenant will check the opposite side.

With Bethlen trailing behind, I slip into the courtyard.

It's an area of roughly a hundred square yards, drenched in shadow and littered with debris, bordered on the east and west by towering crenellated walls. Its northern side is dominated by a gatehouse, comprised of twin guard towers flanking a second raised portcullis. It's through this final gateway that one gains entrance to the castle proper.

I scan the area for movement. Nothing. But there's *something* about the courtyard that disturbs me. I can't quite put a finger on it; it just doesn't feel right. But I've got a job to do, and so I make my way through the shadows, moving stealthily around shattered barrels and stone, my eyes alert for any sudden movement.

I'm making good progress. Then a terrible revelation dawns upon me, forcing me to stop in mid-stride. I finally realise why the courtyard unsettles me: it has been designed for one purpose – to trap intruders. If the outer portcullis were ever breached, an enemy would find themselves bottled within this area. They would then be subjected to raking crossfire from archers positioned in the flanking battlements and gate towers.

In short, it's a death trap!

And here I am, skirting around its perimeter, an open target for any marksman hiding on the battlements – or rather, a target for any witch to cast a spell upon. This is not a good situation to be in. Not good at all. I need to reassess my strategy here. Rather than focus on the courtyard,

I need to monitor the flanking battlements and gatehouse. That's where an attack will come from.

I continue to move forward, but with my eyes trained on the merlons, rising like broken tombstones along the western wall and the northern gatehouse. I gesture back at Bethlen to do the same. But he flicks a hand at me dismissively, annoyed, as if he's already aware of the predicament and that I have no right to be offering him advice.

The situation is hopeless. There could be any number of witches up there, watching our every step. They could launch an attack at any moment. We'd be struck down faster than lame rabbits in a wolves' lair.

I move fast through the courtyard until I'm only a few yards away from the relative safety of the second portcullis, sheltered between the flanking gate towers. Only a dozen more steps and I'll be there. But some sixth sense warns me that I'm being watched.

I stop dead in my tracks.

My head snaps to the left. It only takes a second to spot the marksman, positioned on the southern end of the western wall, his rifle trained directly on me.

CHAPTER
SEVEN

I cry out to Lieutenant Blodklutt and Bethlen, warning them of the ambush. And then I freeze, not knowing what to do, my body unresponsive. After what seems to be an eternity, I dive to the right, into the cover provided by a three-foot-high pile of rubble. Climbing to my feet, I aim my pistol at the marksman. It's not an easy shot at this range, particularly when I've never fired a pistol before in my life. My carbine – being a medium-range weapon – would be more suitable, but I don't have time to ready it.

At least thirty yards – that's the distance to the sniper. An almost impossible shot with a pistol for a trained marksman, let alone a sixteen-year-old boy who's spent his life caring for horses. But I have no other option, for Death has me in its sights. I can't believe the marksman has not yet fired. I'm expecting a sharp report any second now; the last thing I'll no doubt hear before my brains are splattered across the courtyard floor.

I steady my aim, apply pressure to the trigger. Before I release, I catch myself. For it's only now I realise that the marksman is wearing a crimson cassock, exactly the same as the one worn by Robert Monro.

Thank God for that. I breathe a sigh of relief. Robert must have exited the front western gate tower and taken position on the barbican battlements. But why does he have his rifle trained on *me*?

My jubilation in learning that the marksman is Robert vanishes, and a terrible thought makes every hair on my body stand on end. I've heard that powerful witches and warlocks have the ability to take possession of people, to force them to perform acts against their will. Has Robert encountered a witch in the front gatehouse and been possessed? Has he been turned into a pawn of evil? A terrifying thought indeed, but in a witch-infested castle, highly probable.

I once heard of a case in England concerning the Witch Finder General, Matthew Hopkins. Hopkins and his witch hunters had tracked a warlock into the sewers beneath York. Things soon turned ugly when the warlock took possession of one of Hopkins's henchmen. The possessed witch hunter and the warlock fought their way past Hopkins's company, escaped from the sewer, and conducted a month-long killing spree throughout the Yorkshire Dales. Hopkins eventually hunted them down and killed them, but not before forty-seven people had been slain.

Imagine how deadly an opponent Robert Monro – a veteran Hexenjäger – would be if he were possessed by the forces of darkness? And to make matters worse, he already has the drop on me.

It's only now, staring down the barrel of Robert's powerful rifle, I notice that the gun is not locked on me at all. Robert is taking aim at something slightly off to my left. Then it dawns on me that, apart from myself, the Lieutenant and Bethlen, there is something *else* down here. Something we obviously failed to see.

Following the aim of Robert's rifle, I spin to the left, just in time to see the impossible happen.

I lower my weapons in disbelief. This cannot be happening!

Three yards off to my left, a hag is emerging from the courtyard floor, rising from the cobblestone paving as if it were nothing more than water. A *witch!* My first encounter with a proper witch. Not some innocent peasant accused of heresy for owning a black cat, but one of the Devil's concubines, trained in the dark arts – a disciple of Hell.

She has emerged only up to her shoulders, but the ghastly image she presents fills me with a dread the likes of which I have never before known; the type of dread that makes hardened soldiers cross themselves and say hasty prayers in preparation for their inevitable deaths. She – if indeed this abomination can be called a *she* – is terrifying. She has eyes like gobs of spittle, and skin the texture of bark and coloured mucus-yellow. Her teeth are as jagged and crooked as broken fence palings, and she emanates a presence of evil that would suffocate even the heart of the Catholic Church in Rome.

To make matters worse, a second witch starts to emerge from the courtyard floor, some three yards off to the right of the first. Only her head has appeared, but her eyes – filled with hatred – send a wave of terror down my spine.

The first witch to appear rises to her knees and clambers closer. She's obviously been involved in some recent conflict, for her left arm has been severed at the elbow. A trail of gore drips across the flagstone paving.

To my great surprise, it's only now that she finally notices me. She hesitates, stares wide-eyed at me, almost as if she's the one who should be afraid.

Staring face to face with this living nightmare, I almost panic and bolt. Some inner strength I never knew I had, however, orders me to stand my ground. Perhaps it's my father's blood, summoning forth some warrior spirit that has been laying dormant in my soul. Perhaps it's some primal instinct of survival that lies deep within all of us. I might also be subconsciously heeding Armand's and Klaus's advice about never allowing a witch to seize the initiative. I don't know what makes me do it, but I suddenly find myself levelling my pistol at the witch's head.

It's at that exact moment, however, that I flinch instinctively at the report of Robert's rifle. His shot hits the witch straight in the heart, forcing her to stagger back, staring in awe at her blasted chest. But she doesn't fall. To my horror, she staggers towards me, her remaining hand reaching out, its withered fingers clawing at the air.

Rooted to the spot in fear, I somehow manage to discharge my firearm at her. There's a powdered flash followed by a deafening *BLAM!*

The witch might as well have been hit by a cannonball, the impact is so great. If I've learned anything from this encounter, it's that witches can indeed fly. She is thrown clear off her feet, her head exploding in a cloud of pink mist. Her body slams into the eastern wall and slumps to the ground. I never thought that the impact of a pistol fired at close range could be so devastating, and I stand there, dumbstruck, staring at the witch's twitching body.

But whereas the first witch was caught off-guard and was dispatched with the use of our firearms, the second witch – which has now clambered out of the courtyard floor – launches herself at me. Still staring at the first witch's now motionless corpse, I don't even have time to ready my rapier before she's all over me in a maelstrom of slashing inch-long fingernails. They tear into me like razors, and within seconds my tabard is shredded and I'm bleeding from over a dozen wounds.

Stumbling back, I try to push her away, but the fury of

her assault is too strong. I call out desperately for Lieutenant Blodklutt – even Bethlen – to come to my rescue. But hearing sounds over to my right, I snap my head around to see that Bethlen is involved in a vicious struggle with two crones. And then there's the Lieutenant, hemmed against the western wall by three more. With my companions fighting for their own lives, I'm going to have to fend for myself.

Determined to end this fight before I'm shredded to death, I manage to pull away from the witch, freeing my sword arm. Then, as the crone tears after me, I step to the side, drawing her past me, and – with a savagery I never knew I possessed – hammer the pommel of my rapier into the side of her head. She recoils, and I lunge forward, pressing the attack, certain my blade will skewer her. But I make the fatal mistake of underestimating her.

Moving with a speed that defies her emaciated appearance, she dodges my thrust, weaves through my defences and tackles me to the ground. Her mouth is like a burst sewer, spitting saliva and blood, as black as oil, all over me, and she's consumed by such a rage that her bloodshot eyes practically pop out of their sockets.

My rapier is useless in such close quarters. Nor can I reach my daggers, for they are tucked in the folds of my boots, and the witch is all over me, pinning me down. And so, in an act of pure desperation, I drive my thumbs into her eyes. She falls back, blinded, allowing me to regain my feet.

Unarmed, and as blind as a bat, she doesn't stand much of a chance defending herself against the sharp edge of a rapier – even one wielded by a novice. A series of savage thrusts brings a decisive conclusion to the struggle.

Even before the witch drops lifeless to the ground, I find myself staggering over to aid Bethlen, driven again, I can only assume, by my father's blood hammering in my veins. Bethlen's already killed one witch, but another has wrestled him to the ground and is trying to gnaw into his neck.

Ten steps and I've crossed to Bethlen. Realising that a fellow Hexenjäger is bearing down upon it, the witch rears its head from Bethlen's neck. It hisses at me like some demonic serpent . . . just as my blade cleaves its head clean off.

I kick the lifeless corpse clear from Bethlen and drag him to his feet. He's bleeding from the neck. It doesn't look like a serious wound, though. Nothing some salve and a bandage won't fix. Rather than thank me and extend a hand in gratitude, he shoots me an enraged look and pushes me away. Did he honestly believe he was going to defeat that witch? A few seconds more and it would have bitten straight through his neck.

Shocked by Bethlen's lack of gratitude, I turn my attention to Lieutenant Blodklutt. He's already dispatched two of the witches. A third is nursing a vicious wound on its left shoulder. But the Lieutenant is unscathed, and I have barely taken two steps when I realise my assistance is hardly needed. Blodklutt weaves forward in a synchronised dance of death, his blade a blur of silver. It's over in a heartbeat.

The final witch slain, we gather in the centre of the courtyard, our backs to one another, weapons at the ready, half expecting the courtyard floor to erupt like Judgement Day. But the only movement comes from the battlements overlooking the courtyard. Robert has reloaded his rifle and is providing cover from the western wall. He's been joined by Klaus and von Frankenthal. Armand and Captain Faust appear on the battlement opposite.

Having issued orders for Klaus and Robert to check the inner gatehouse, Captain Faust, accompanied by Armand and von Frankenthal, makes his way down to the courtyard. As Lieutenant Blodklutt goes over to report what happened, I wander off to a quiet corner. The rush of adrenaline subsides, leaving me with a shocking awareness of how bloody the skirmish was and how lucky I am to have survived. A sickness wells in my stomach and my sword-arm starts to tremble. Not wanting my companions to see me in this state, I turn my back towards them and try to fight back the feeling of nausea.

Not long has passed before I become aware of a massive presence behind me.

'I told you to stay out of combat,' von Frankenthal scolds, noticing the blood on my hands and the torn state of my clothes. 'You want to be a hero, go ahead. But don't expect to make it out of here alive. Who do you think you are – Alejandro de la Cruz?'

De la Cruz is a living legend – a nineteen-year-old Spaniard who has risen to the rank of Captain within one year of joining the Hexenjäger. I've never met him, but I'd have a purse full of gold if I were to receive a coin for every time I've heard his name mentioned around Burg Grimmheim.

I'm so focused on fighting back the sensation of nausea that I'm hardly aware of my reply. 'Punishing me for Gerhard's death will not bring him back.'

Before I know what's happening, von Frankenthal grabs me, spins me around, and pins me – hard – against the courtyard wall. 'Don't you dare mention his name again. Ever!'

His eyes are blazing with rage, and for a moment I fear he might smash my head against the wall. But then he gives me a final shove and stalks off, leaving me rubbing my neck, wondering how I managed to muster the nerve to criticise him.

Armand was correct when he said that von Frankenthal has a lot of pent-up anger concerning Gerhard's death. But he can't go on blaming himself for what happened. Nor will I allow him to keep venting his anger at me. He has, when all is said and done, been assigned to protect me during this mission. Even if it means risking personal injury, I must make von Frankenthal accept his new charge – make him accept responsibility for my safety. I don't

71

know exactly how I'll go about achieving this, but I have to start somewhere.

Surprisingly, the encounter with von Frankenthal has distracted my thoughts from the fight with the witches and quelled my nausea. In an effort to keep my mind off the horrific skirmish, I start to clean my bloodied blade on the tattered remnants of my tabard. Not long has passed when I look up to see Armand standing before me.

'Let's get those wounds bandaged,' he says and, with a flask of water, a phial of pungent salve and some makeshift bandages, he starts to tend my wounds. 'You'll be sore for a few days, that's for sure, but there's nothing serious here. You'll live. Nobody comes out unscathed from their first encounter with a witch.'

'You're just being polite,' I say dismally, wincing in pain as a bandage is applied to my right arm. 'I bet you weren't injured.'

'I've got a scar that will argue otherwise.' Armand pulls back his sleeve, revealing a pearl-grey scar running the length of his left forearm. 'Compliments of the first witch I ever fought. You'll find all of the Hexenjäger – even Blod-klutt – bear such trophies.'

Whereas Armand is proud of his scar, considering it a memento of his initiation, I wish I could erase the memory of the skirmish from my mind forever. I never again want to be reminded of this horrific ordeal. I fear, however, that even though my scars will heal and eventually fade, the experience is going to haunt me for the rest of my life.

'I think I've made a big mistake,' I say. 'I don't belong here. I don't have what it takes to become a witch hunter. I thought I could be a soldier like my father, but I was wrong.'

I'm even about to tell Armand that my letter of introduction was fake, that I lied about being a junior officer under Montecuccoli, that I have never seen a battlefield in my life. But before I have a chance to confess, Armand grabs me by the shoulders and forces me to look into his eyes.

'You told me before that your motive for joining the Hexenjäger was to answer an inner call,' he says. 'Well, I think you may have found your calling. Blodklutt reported that you slew three witches. No initiate has ever done that – not even De la Cruz. I've also heard that you came to the defence of Bethlen and saved his life. That's an impressive start for someone with so little training in the art of killing witches. There's more to you than meets the eye, Jakob von Drachenfels. What you lack in skill with your blade, you make up for in spirit, and that's something that no amount of training can provide. You might only be sixteen, but there's the spirit of a warrior within you.' He releases his grip on my shoulders and his eyes soften in their intensity. 'You mentioned your father before. Tell me about him.'

I shake my head and sigh. 'There's not much to tell. He died when I was four. All I know is that he was a soldier – a cavalry commander, in fact – who fought in the Low Countries, hiring his sword out as a mercenary for the Spanish. I even know he spent some time in Castile. But that's all I know.'

Armand looks at me square in the eye. 'He'd be proud of you. And I'm sure his spirit lies within you.' He pauses, twists an end of his moustache in thought. 'I may know someone who might be able to shed some light upon his life. It's a long shot, and I certainly don't want you to get your hopes too high, but one of our order, a man by the name of Dietrich Hommel, served in the Low Countries some fifteen years ago. He was part of a German cavalry unit. As I said, you shouldn't get too hopeful, for thousands of German soldiers fought alongside the Spanish in the Netherlands. But I suppose it's a start.'

Armand's words strike a tender chord in my heart, filling a void I never believed could be filled. Could it be that I might finally begin to find some answers as to who my father really was?

'I also believe that if your father were alive today he would have joined the Hexenjäger,' Armand continues. 'You must remember that we are the first line of defence against an evil that threatens to engulf our world. Like it or not, it is out there, lurking in the shadows, and it grows stronger with each passing day. And it's people like you and I who will drive back the darkness, protecting all that is good. I believe we have all been given the gift of life in order to fulfil a specific purpose. I've spent my entire life searching for my purpose, and I still haven't found it. But it looks to me as if you may have just discovered yours.'

Armand's conviction and passion stir something deep within me. The thought of leaving the Hexenjäger is momentarily swept aside. Again, I find myself imagining that the Hexenjäger is the contemporary equivalent of the military orders of old – Christian warriors defending the borders of the Holy Land against the forces of evil. But this time the stakes are higher. This time we aren't fighting the Infidel, but the Devil's legions. Granted, it's dangerous work, but no cause has ever been so just.

'Besides, I think we'll be going in as one unit from here on,' Armand says, noticing the effect his words are having on me. 'I'll be able to keep an eye out for you. So what am I to do? Am I to go over to Captain Faust and report that you're planning a mutiny? Or am I to report that we have one of the finest witch hunters in the making over here?'

I can't help but smile. 'I'm hardly planning a mutiny. And, yes, you've managed to convince me to stay.'

Armand puts an arm around my shoulder and escorts me back to the others. 'You know, you had me worried there for a while. And don't worry about Revelation 6.8. He has nothing personal against you. Besides, you can't leave this order. Who else will I have to talk to – Bethlen?'

'Talking about Bethlen, why does he resent me so much?' I ask, wondering if Armand can shed any light on the topic. 'I saved his life just now, and he looked at me as if he wished I were dead. I don't understand him at all.'

Armand shrugs, looks over at Bethlen. 'I consider myself a good judge of character, but I cannot read people's minds. Have you ever tried talking to him, asked him why he dislikes you?'

I shake my head. 'No, but I might follow your advice.'

We rejoin the rest of our team and start to reload and ready our weapons. I can't help but notice the resentful look Bethlen is throwing my way. My confidence bolstered by Armand's encouraging words, I decide it's time to find out what lies at the heart of Bethlen's resentment towards me.

'That was some fight,' I say, trying to initiate conversation.

Bethlen looks me up and down, his upper lip curled in distaste. He grunts, turns his back on me, and continues to clean his blade.

'I know you might not want to talk right now, but there's something I need to know,' I press, my voice kept low so that the others can't hear. 'It's no secret that you don't like me. But what have I ever done to offend you? I know I'm only an initiate, and have yet to prove my value to this order. But I can't help feeling you genuinely dislike me. I saved your life back there, and yet you couldn't even bring yourself to thank me. Why?'

'I resent everything you stand for,' Bethlen says, his back still turned to me, his words laced with malice. 'Why don't you just go back to the kitchens – to that girl you're always talking to?'

I look at him incredulously. 'Everything I stand for? But you don't even know me. And don't drag Sabina into this.'

Bethlen smiles maliciously. 'There's no need to get defensive, whelp. And don't worry about your precious little lady friend – I'll remember to tell her that you died. Don't worry about that. It will give me great pleasure to console her. Rest assured, I'll give her all the care and love she needs.'

'She's just a friend,' I say, nonetheless sickened by the mere thought of Bethlen going near Sabina. 'What have I ever done to you?'

'I know that you sauntered into our order carrying a letter of introduction.' Bethlen snaps around and points an accusing finger at me. 'And I've heard that you served under Generalissimo Montecuccoli. Wasn't that commission good enough for you? Did you need to come here to show off your letter and make the rest of us feel like dirt?'

'What? I don't think you –'

'People like you have had everything handed to you on silver platters,' Bethlen interrupts, not allowing me a chance to explain myself. 'I, on the other hand, have had to work hard to get to where I am. Whereas you've simply clicked your fingers and everything has been given to you, I've had to use my own cunning and brawn to earn my position. I never even knew who my father was. I was raised in Mannheim's crime-infested alleyways. I've had to work – hard – my entire life to get where I am. And that, whelp, is why I dislike you and your French friend so much. You represent all that is wrong with this world, with its lucky few born into prestige and wealth, whilst the rest of us have to fight for the scraps from your table.'

He stalks off, leaving me stunned, staring at the empty space where he had been standing. For the first time in the past week, I feel genuine pity – rather than resentment – for Bethlen. But his animosity is misplaced. I'm not from an extremely wealthy family. Yes, my uncle and aunt are well-respected and wealthy by some standards, but they are certainly not landed gentry. My uncle has had to work hard his entire life to establish a reputation as a skilled farrier, and it has only been during the past ten years that he has started to reap the rewards of his labour. The only time I ever left Dresden was to accompany a family friend, Father Giuseppe Callumbro – a Benedictine monk who taught me how to read and write Italian and Latin – on a pilgrimage to Saint Peter's Basilica in Rome. But I can't tell Bethlen the truth about my past, or that I have no military experience. He'd report my deception to the Grand Hexenjäger, resulting in my immediate expulsion.

Bethlen and I are similar in more ways than he could

begin to imagine. Had it not been for my uncle, who took me in after the death of my mother, I could have become Bethlen – a street-urchin, eking out a living by sleight of hand and cunning.

I'm drawn from my thoughts by Captain Faust, who comes over and inspects my wounds. He pats me on the shoulder, an unspoken acknowledgement of the role I played in the skirmish, then returns to the centre of the courtyard.

'Five minutes, gentlemen,' he announces. 'Then we move again. And be on your guard. Those witches used transmutation spells to rise out of the ground. There's no telling what we are going to run into.'

I pull out one of the wooden gunpowder containers attached to my bandolier and start to reload my pistol. But some morbid fascination compels me to glance at the first witch I slew. She's lying in a crumpled heap over by the far wall. I don't feel my stomach turn when I look at her. Nor do I feel any pity or remorse. There's now just a cold emptiness within me. Perhaps I have the making of a witch hunter after all.

And it's only now I recall that, when the witch emerged from the ground, one of her arms had been severed, leaving a bleeding stump. Someone – or *something* – had only recently cut it off.

I feel the skin crawl on the back of my neck. Some sixth sense warns me that something is not quite right.

'We are missing something here,' I say, drawing everyone's attention. 'These witches weren't waiting in ambush. They were just as surprised to see us as we were to see them. One of them even bore a fresh wound, its arm having been severed. They were fleeing from something – something that put the fear of God into them.'

Von Frankenthal is standing guard in the shadows under the second portcullis. He looks like some behemoth guarding the gates of Hell. I can clearly understand why Armand has given him the nickname Revelation 6.8.

'What?' he says, his eyes narrowing with intrigue. 'Are you suggesting there's someone *else* in here? Fighting the witches?'

'Well, if there is, it certainly makes our job a lot easier,' Armand says. 'But who do you think would . . . ?'

'Listen!' von Frankenthal warns.

A sudden silence. We all look at von Frankenthal. There's nothing at first. Then we all hear it: sounds of combat, coming from deep within the castle, so faint they can barely be heard. But we can distinguish musket fire and agonising screams.

After a minute or so, the sounds fade into a pervasive silence.

We exchange bewildered looks. What on earth is going on?

CHAPTER EIGHT

'The Devil take us. Someone else *is* in here,' Bethlen says.

I cast a suspicious eye at Bethlen. Maybe I'm wrong, but his surprised tone seemed feigned, almost as if he's privy to some secret information. Nobody else seems to have noticed this, however, so I focus on the more pressing concern of trying to determine who else is in the castle.

Armand kneels by one of the slain witches and conducts a crude autopsy on the body in a vain attempt to determine who dealt the initial wounds. 'Any guesses as to who it might be?'

'Rather than that, we should ask ourselves what they are after,' Captain Faust says.

Armand's head snaps up. 'The Scourge of Jericho! But surely not.'

'What else would anybody be doing here?' Captain Faust returns. 'They have to be after the relic.'

'But how would anybody other than the Hexenjäger know of the resting place of the trumpet?' Armand questions. 'We've only just learned of its location. Even if there were a spy within our order – which I pray to God there isn't – there wouldn't have been time to pass the information on to anybody else. We were dispatched from Burg Grimmheim only yesterday morning.'

'We discovered the relic's hiding place. That doesn't mean that others haven't,' von Frankenthal says, tapping the hilt of his rapier in anticipation of combat, his tone as ominous as a death knell.

Searching for religious artefacts and selling holy relics has been an obsession of the Catholic Church since the Dark Ages. In medieval times an interested buyer could purchase anything from splinters from the True Cross and bones from Jesus's fingers. Demand was greater than supply. Consequently, forgeries were rife. I once heard of a case in which two dozen 'authentic' Holy Grails were sold by the same monk, all from within the same market square, and all within three hours.

But the churches of Europe were determined to monopolise possession of authentic artefacts. And so, relic hunters wandered Christendom and the Holy Land. Some, consumed by religious fervour, were commissioned by the Church. Others were mercenaries who sold their treasure to the highest bidder. Irrespective of their motive, however, they were all skilful warriors and deadly opponents. And some of them still exist today, now all but relics of a former age, like the very treasure they seek.

'My guess is either relic hunters or witch hunters,' I say, as if I'm the experienced one who knows all about these matters; a regular authority on the subject. Normally I'd leave discussions of this nature to the professionals, but my confidence has been bolstered by the fact that I've dispatched three witches. 'Klaus told me that a company of witch hunters was sent into these mountains last year. Perhaps another company has been sent to find what happened to them. Their search may have brought them here.'

'I'd say the lad is right,' Klaus says. 'And if they are witch hunters, it will be to our advantage. They won't want the trumpet, but only to eliminate the coven. I'm sure they'll assist us. But if they are relic hunters, then we have a problem.'

'We don't just have a problem. It's *far* worse than that.' Armand's been prying with a dagger into one of the witches. I've been wondering what he's been up to, but trying not to focus too much on the gruesome scene. Now, finally, he extracts something from the gunshot wound he's been investigating. 'You're not going to like this.'

He wipes the blood from the object and holds it up.

It's a silver pistol ball, with a crucifix carved on it.

Armand might well have announced that the Pope is a blasphemous Lutheran, such is the stunned reaction of the Hexenjäger. I can't help but notice, however, that Lieutenant Blodklutt and Captain Faust exchange a knowing glance, as if they're not too surprised by this discovery.

The significance of the silver pistol ball, however, means nothing to me.

Armand notices my blank look. 'Only one group uses such balls,' he explains, then pauses, stares me hard in the eyes. I can tell this is going to be one hell of a punch. 'The Brotherhood of the Cross!'

I stare back, stunned, suddenly feeling weak in the knees. God help us!

The Brotherhood of the Cross. I doubt there's one person in all of the Holy Roman Empire who has not heard of them. Three fanatical Protestants. Also known as the Holy Trinity, but wrapped in black cloaks like the Devil's ravens.

The Father: Leopold von Wolfenbüttel. His wife and six daughters were accused of heresy and burned alive at the stake. Since that fateful day he's been fuelled by a personal vendetta against the Catholic Church. He's conducted a reign of terror in Lorraine, crucified ten parish priests in Sondershausen, and tortured to death over a hundred Catholics in the Kyfhäuser Mountains.

The Son: Kurt von Wolfenbüttel. The sole son of Leopold. A puritanical maniac. Only the plague is said to have killed more people. He's as powerful as a galloping draught horse. It's said that he cannot be killed, having survived over two dozen musket and sword wounds. He keeps a tally of his kills by scarring his forearm with a heated blade. Strangely, he paints his face white before going into combat.

The Holy Spirit: a shadowy figure. Identity unknown. Where he appears, death follows.

In short, not the sort of people you want to meet. Not unless you want to be strapped on a bolting horse and delivered to the nearest graveyard.

There's an uncomfortable silence. All I can hear is Bethlen squeezing air through his nostrils and Armand clicking his tongue. It's a rather annoying habit, that. I've noticed that Armand tends to do it when in deep thought. I don't know if he's even aware he's doing it. But now isn't the right moment to draw attention to his idiosyncrasies. I don't want to distract him from his thoughts, for we need a solution to our present predicament. Indeed, our situation has just become so dire that we might as well have been sent into Hell without even a crucifix.

'It's safe to assume they are after the trumpet.' Captain Faust is as solemn as a Papal Inquisitor with a migraine. 'And you can imagine the havoc they'll wreak if they get their hands on it. They'd go straight for the heart of the Roman Catholic Church – the Vatican. They would plunge

Europe into a war the likes of which we've never seen before. It would be a full-scale war between Catholics and Protestants – Armageddon for Christendom.'

'Then we have to stop them at all costs,' Bethlen says.

'But that's easier said than done,' Lieutenant Blodklutt remarks dryly.

I swallow nervously. It hardly inspires confidence when someone of his fighting ability has doubts.

'So do we let the Brotherhood do the hard work for us?' Armand asks. 'Let them take out the witches, brave the dungeon and collect the trumpet? All we'd have to do is intercept them when they emerge with the prize.'

'As nice as that sounds, it's too risky,' Captain Faust comments. 'We can't run the risk of letting them get anywhere near the trumpet. On the contrary, we must go in after them. It's easiest to kill a wolf when it's already distracted. The Brotherhood will not be expecting us. We have the element of surprise and the advantage of numbers. They may have already suffered a loss at the hands of the witches. We'll sneak up from behind, wait for them to engage the coven. Then we'll catch them by surprise. This may be our only chance to put an end to their unholy war.'

He makes it sound so simple – as easy as eating a piece of pie. But I fear this pie has been laced with arsenic, and we've just been delivered a double serve.

⚔CHAPTER
NINE

When the other Hexenjäger return from checking the inner gatehouse, we gather in the shadows under the second portcullis, noting the layout of the castle, strategising our plan of attack.

A central courtyard opens before us, almost fifty yards wide and just as long. Along its southern, western and eastern flanks, adjoining the battlement walls, are a series of store-houses, guard rooms and stables. All appear empty, silent. To the north stands the stronghold of the castle: a central keep, six storeys high, towering over the other buildings, entered via a nail-studded door that faces onto the court-yard. Somewhere beneath it lies the dungeon and Countess Gretchen Kraus's lair – the lair of the Blood Countess.

Captain Faust directs Robert to take position in the highest point of the castle – a tower, even taller than the central keep, rising from the eastern battlement. It's obviously an observation post, used to detect the approach of an enemy over a thousand yards away. But Robert will use it to monitor the *interior* of the castle. Overlooking the central courtyard, the castle's battlements and the windows on the eastern and southern sides of the keep, the tower is a perfect sniping post.

It was only a week ago, when I was first assigned to cleaning the Hexenjäger's arsenal of guns and blades, that I first saw a rifle. Three were stacked on a rack along the rear wall of the armoury, separate from the dozens of other pistols, carbines and muskets that lined the walls of the room, and I was tempted to spend some time analysing them. Like flintlock muskets, they are muzzle loaders, but they are considerably longer and have rifled barrels, giving the ball far greater accuracy. I've heard that they are accurate up to two hundred yards. That's far better than my carbine, which I've been told has an effective range of no more than forty yards.

And there's no questioning Robert's skill with the rifle. He shot the witch in the courtyard directly in the heart. It's certainly reassuring knowing that he'll be monitoring our progress and watching our backs. It will be like having our own guardian angel.

With Robert providing cover, we are to move straight into the central keep. We're to ignore the buildings along the perimeter of the courtyard. This time we're to go straight in – to follow the sounds of combat until we find the Brotherhood. Until then, no firearms are to be discharged within the keep. We are to use only our blades. Captain Faust doesn't want to risk giving away our element of surprise. Only Robert has permission to fire, but as a last resort.

After a few words with Captain Faust, the Scot scurries off into the inner gatehouse, making his way to the tower. Once he's in position, we'll move into the keep. Blodklutt and Armand will lead. Armand has already drawn both of his cavalry sabres, and is bragging about how he will be the one to bring down Kurt von Wolfenbüttel. Lieutenant Blodklutt, on the other hand, doesn't say a word, his brooding eyes locked on the keep, searching for movement through its windows. He is determined and focused, like an Inquisitor scanning the flesh of some terrified peasant for moles or other signs of devilry.

I can't see a thing. There's no movement, no sounds – nothing. You'd never guess we'd heard sounds of combat come from there only moments before. It's as though there hasn't been a living creature enter the keep for over a hundred years.

But somewhere within there lurk three of the most dangerous men alive. And any second now we'll be going in after them.

⟁CHAPTER⟁
TEN

A white handkerchief appears from one of the windows of the tower, indicating Robert Monro is in position. Not a second later, Lieutenant Blodklutt and Armand race forward, making a direct line for the keep's nail-studded door. They are halfway across the courtyard when we break our cover and follow after them.

Keeping my head low, I sprint across the open expanse, conscious of the noise made by my jostling weapons and bandolier. I'm expecting a cry of alarm to be sounded at any second, warning the witches within the keep of our presence. To my relief, none is given, and I reach the keep only a few seconds behind Armand and Lieutenant Blodklutt, who have already slipped through the door and entered the building. I try to listen over the sounds made by my other companions as they race across the courtyard.

But there are no cries of alarm from within the keep; no squeal of steel on steel, no blood-choked cries. The coast seems clear.

I make the sign of the cross, say a quick prayer, and swallow back the boulder in my throat. Then, when the others reach the door, we enter the keep.

We move into the darkness beyond the door, the swish of our boots across the flagstone floor reverberating off the walls. The air is so stale it almost makes me gag. It smells of ancient stone and dust, like a tomb that has just been opened for the first time in centuries.

My eyes gradually adjust to the darkness, revealing a corridor stretching before me, a series of doors spanning off it. At the end of the corridor lies a stairwell, winding up into darkness. Lieutenant Blodklutt and Armand have already advanced halfway down the corridor. They are moving with the stealth of stalking cats, checking each doorway, ensuring each room is empty before moving forward.

A massive figure stirs by my side: Christian von Frankenthal. Even when he's crouching he still towers over me. He's not really built for stealth, and was probably sired by a pair of battering rams. He's moving silently, nonetheless.

We fan out across the corridor and move steadily towards the stairwell. There's no sign of the witches, nor of the Brotherhood of the Cross. There's nothing in any of the rooms but dust and cobwebs. Then, in the final room, we find them – two witches, as old as Eve, no more than husks in rags. They are sprawled across the floor, lying in pools of blood, both killed by single pistol shots to the head.

'Precise,' Klaus whispers, entering the room and kneeling over their bodies. 'Shot square in the forehead. No other wounds on them. No signs of struggle. They were taken out quickly.'

Whilst Captain Faust and von Frankenthal enter the room to inspect the bodies, I stay by the doorway and avert my eyes, sickened by the scene. As Klaus moves back from the witches – and my other companions are either standing outside in the corridor, or are focusing on the dead bodies – a malicious smile crosses his lips. It lasts only a fleeting second, but it lasts long enough for me to realise that there is a sinister side to his nature. If I am not mistaken, he has taken a perverse pleasure in seeing the slain witches. I also cannot help but feel, however, that there was a hint of familiarity in his smile, as if he has witnessed this type of scene many times before, and was admiring the marksmanship of the person who had shot the witches.

'Looks like the work of Kurt,' Captain Faust observes, drawing my attention. 'He's an expert shot. Never misses. Single pistol shot to the forehead is his speciality.'

'We might be about to meet him. Someone – or *something* – approaches.'

That's the last thing on earth I wanted Armand to say. He's crouched in the stairwell, his eyes dancing with excitement. He raises a finger to his lips, indicates silence, then points up the stairs.

We scurry forward and halt in the stairwell, listening for what has alerted Armand. About a minute passes before, from somewhere above us, we hear scraping footfalls. It's hard to tell exactly which level they are coming from. Sound resonates in here like an accidentally dropped Bible in church during the Lord's Prayer. But it's certainly not coming from the floor directly above us. My guess is several floors up.

BLAM!

A firearm discharges. I jump so high it's a miracle my head doesn't smash into the ceiling. The sound, reverberating down the stairwell, is deafening, like firing a cannon in a confessional box. It's followed by sounds of a scuffle: the swish of a blade, and an agonised scream, almost inhuman in its blood-gargled terror. Then we hear rushing feet and snatches of panicked voices. Coming down the stairwell.

Coming straight towards us!

We retreat back down the corridor. Captain Faust divides us into two groups and instructs us to disperse into two rooms on opposite sides of the corridor. We are to then wait in ambush. If it turns out to be witches, we are to let them pass. We don't want to alert the Brotherhood of our presence and give away the element of surprise. But if it's the Brotherhood, we will spring our trap. Caught between the witches and our blades, and trapped within the narrow confines of the corridor, we should be able to cut them down.

I barely dare breathe for fear of giving away our position. As God is my witness, I have never before felt so afraid. It feels as if I have a cannonball lodged in my throat, and I give a nervous gulp. I then spare a quick glance over my shoulder. I'm in the room with the dead witches. I hope that's not a premonition of what befalls this room's occupants.

Armand, Klaus and Captain Faust are positioned in front of me, their weapons poised, crouched like a pack of wolves hunting the scent of death.

'Get ready. They're coming,' Captain Faust whispers. 'If it's the Brotherhood, let them pass before we attack. Pistols first. Then we close with blades.'

Thank God for that. I am dreading the thought of being involved in another vicious hand-to-hand fight. The last witch I fought was too fast, latching herself onto me before I had time to ready my rapier. I won't make that mistake again. These pistols are going to make sure that no witch – or member of the Brotherhood of the Cross – is going to come within ten yards of me.

Armand licks his lips in anticipation of combat, like a dog salivating before a meal. 'Remember – Kurt is mine,' he whispers.

'Don't be too eager,' Klaus warns, as cool as chilled wine. 'Many men have dreamed of killing him. They are now all buried under six feet of earth.'

Armand snickers recklessly in return, as if this chapter in history is already written, his victory over Kurt von Wolfenbüttel assured. He looks back at me.

'As promised, I'll do my best to guard over you,' he whispers. 'Don't rush in after me. Stay back and use your pistols.'

I hold them before me. 'Believe me, you don't need to tell me that.'

I barely have time to check they are readied before the corridor erupts with frenzied movement.

Our quarry has exited the stairwell.

My head snaps up, my muscles as tense as a drawn bow string as someone bolts past our room. Terrified, I nonetheless try to peer past my companions in an attempt to see who – or *what* – it is. But I'm stopped by Armand. He draws back one of his sabres, holding me in position, indicating I'm to wait.

There's the sound of more rushing feet. It's obviously the witches, otherwise Captain Faust, standing closest to the door, would have sprung the trap. He remains as fixed as one of the Pope's Swiss Guards on sentry duty.

A few heartbeats pass. All goes deathly quiet; then we hear movement again. Only this time, the sound is distinctly different. There's no panic but measured steps in leather-soled boots. They pause at the base of the stairwell, almost as if assessing the situation. Over a minute passes before they move forward again.

But this time with stealth, and stopping just short of our room.

CHAPTER ELEVEN

This has suddenly developed into my worst nightmare. As far as I know, Kurt von Wolfenbüttel – the man who cannot be *killed* – is standing on the opposite side of the wall I'm hiding behind. I can picture him in my mind, the features of his white-painted face twisted in savage fury, his weapons drawn, waiting to tear into us like a wolf about to launch into a chicken coop.

So what do we do now? Simply stand here and wait for the Brotherhood to burst into our room? Or do we leap out, salvaging what remains of our element of surprise?

The tension's so palpable you could scoop it into a bucket and sell it off as soup. I don't even dare swallow lest the noise give away our position. You have to admire my companions, though, particularly Captain Faust. He hasn't moved a muscle. I've seen statues that are more animated.

It's just then, however, that the Captain does stir. He cranes his head forward, tries to hear what's happening in the corridor. Barely a second passes before he snaps his head back to look at us, his eyes wide in alarm. He flicks back his rapier, ushering us deeper into the room.

We have barely shuffled back four steps before we hear the sound that has alarmed Captain Faust – a soft hissing sound. My mind has barely had time to register the implications of this before *it* is lobbed into the room – a cannonball, with an ignited fuse!

Grenades have been in use for some time now. I recall reading that one had been used during a skirmish at Hampstead Bridge during the English Civil War. In that instance, a single grenade repelled a cavalry charge, destroyed the bridge, and took the life of the poor soldier who lit it.

They are essentially a hollowed cannonball shell filled with gunpowder and ignited by a wick. Arguably one of the most destructive weapons invented.

Up until now, I have never before seen one. And I can think of a million ways I'd rather see my first. Having one lobbed into the room you are standing in isn't exactly a comforting experience.

Klaus, Armand and Captain Faust are one step ahead of me. No sooner have I had the thought of being splattered all over the walls than we are bolting for the room's window. I've never seen men move so fast. It all happens so quickly, in fact, that for a moment I forget how high up we are, and I almost cry out in warning to my companions. But then I remember that we are still on the ground floor, and the next instant I find myself diving out the window after them.

Scrambling to our feet, we sprint for our lives. Armand moves over to my side, tries to shield me from the imminent explosion.

We have only cleared ten yards when – *BOOM!* – the explosion rips through the room behind us. It tears a gaping hole through the exterior wall, knocking us off our feet, showering us in debris and filling the air with smoke.

Along with Armand and Captain Faust, I clamber to my feet. My head's swimming so much I can barely stand. It feels as though I've been sideswiped by a carriage. Out of the corner of my eye, however, I notice that Klaus hasn't moved. He's lying prostrate on the ground, covered in rubble.

I reach for my discarded pistols, then head over towards Klaus. I've almost reached his side when I notice that his eyes are wide open, staring up at me lifelessly.

I stop dead in my tracks. The revelation that Klaus has not survived the explosion hits me like a sledge-hammer. Only a second ago he was sprinting by my side. And now he's lying there, bloodied and torn – *dead*.

Dazed from the explosion, and shocked by the sudden loss of one of my companions, I turn to look back at the room, just in time to see a gloved hand, brandishing a flint-lock pistol, emerge through the smoke.

I freeze.

From the smoke-engulfed room a face materialises, painted white, twisted in savage hatred.

Kurt von Wolfenbüttel!

He takes aim with his pistol. But we're packed so close together – helping each other scramble to our feet and collecting our weapons – it's impossible to tell who he's aiming at. I can only hope that the smoke will spoil his aim. But I fear we don't stand a chance, not at this range.

Not even Armand has his defences ready. He's wiping blood from a deep gash on his neck, his sabres lying where he dropped them, his face as smudged and dirtied as a street urchin who's been bobbing for apples in the city dump.

I don't even have time to raise my pistols before – *BLAM!* – von Wolfenbüttel's gun erupts in a powdered flash. Fearing I may have been the target of his shot, I flinch instinctively, clutch my chest, at the gaping wound I expect to find there. But I'm amazed to find that there is no wound.

My relief turns to horror when I catch movement in the corner of my eye. Someone staggers forward, their hat torn from their head by the impact of the pistol ball that has smashed through their skull.

My jaw drops in disbelief as Captain Faust drops dead to the courtyard floor.

CHAPTER TWELVE

I stand dumbstruck, staring at Captain Faust's still form, struggling to come to terms with not only the death of another of my companions, but the death of our commanding officer.

Armand, however, doesn't miss a beat. Captain Faust has barely hit the ground before he retrieves his sabres, races forward and engages von Wolfenbüttel – who has just drawn his blade and emerged through the hole in the wall – in a savage duel.

I snap back to reality. Now is not the right time to grieve for the fallen. Not when still on the battlefield, and particularly not when Armand may be in need of my assistance. And so, not wanting to risk the possibility of shooting Armand, I tuck my pistols into my belt, draw my rapier and sprint over to Armand's side.

Von Wolfenbüttel is a behemoth, taller and wider than Christian von Frankenthal. He looks like a titan from Greek legend, as powerful as the Bastille, his face more scarred than a butcher's chopping board – evidence of the many wounds he has endured; testimony that this man cannot be killed.

'Let me help you,' I say, but at a complete loss as to what assistance I can offer the French duellist.

Armand shakes his head vehemently, presses the attack. 'No. He's too dangerous an opponent. Stand back.'

Armand can warn me all he wants, but not even a dozen stallions would be enough to drag me away from this fight. I've already seen two of my companions slain by von Wolfenbüttel. I'm not going to allow him to kill Armand and record his death as a scar on his forearm. Besides, I'll stand no chance whatsoever in trying to fight von Wolfenbüttel single-handedly. And so, ignoring Armand, my confidence bolstered by the fact that I have already slain three witches, I skirt behind the behemoth, waiting for an opening to appear.

But von Wolfenbüttel is no fool and knows exactly what I'm trying to do. He keeps mobile, moving with a dexterity that defies his massive frame. He darts to the left, springs to the right, then shifts back to the left again, not allowing me to attack him in his exposed flank – or blind spot.

Armand, however, is determined to go for a quick kill. Perhaps this is dictated by the fact that he fears for my safety and wishes to kill von Wolfenbüttel before I am injured. I'm sure he's also being driven by his bloodlust and desire to enact revenge for the death of his companions. He feigns to his left, then darts back to the right, lightning-fast, catching von Wolfenbüttel off-balance. One of Armand's sabres then snakes out at von Wolfenbüttel's thighs. At the same instant, I lunge forward, my heart pounding, my rapier aimed at the exposed left-hand side of von Wolfenbüttel's chest.

This should do it. If these thrusts don't kill von Wolfenbüttel they will at least leave him maimed. It will then only be a matter of time before we bring him down. But any sense of victory is short-lived, for we have underestimated our opponent.

Just as our blades are about to hit their targets, von Wolfenbüttel regains his balance, as if it were a ploy to lure us in, committing us to attacks that would leave our own defences open. Before I know what has happened, von Wolfenbüttel becomes a blur of motion, launching himself in the air. Armand's sabre slashes harmlessly beneath his feet. Twisting in mid-air, von Wolfenbüttel parries my blade, then delivers an impossibly fast riposte to my chest. At the same instant, his right foot lashes out, slamming into Armand's face with the force of a rifle butt.

By the time von Wolfenbüttel's feet find the ground, Armand lays sprawled on the cobblestone floor, senseless, and I'm staggering back, a cut to my left shoulder.

It all happened within the blink of an eye. Impossible!

I never knew anybody could wield a sword with such blinding speed. Von Wolfenbüttel would rival even Lieutenant Blodklutt.

What chance do Armand and I possibly have in defeating him? Practically none, particularly now that he has the advantage. And he does not hesitate in seizing it. Within a heartbeat he's taken two strides. He stands over Armand, his blade drawn back in preparation to deliver a death thrust, the coup de grâce.

Armand lays dazed on the ground, spitting blood, unaware of the nightmare looming over him. But von Wolfenbüttel hesitates for a second – like a child considering an insect it's about to kill.

And in that second I act, snatching a pistol from my belt. I don't even have time to take aim before I squeeze the trigger. There's a powdered flash and a deafening report. My hand is thrown back by the recoil, bringing a blinding pain to my wounded left shoulder.

Then I hear a cry. But it's not a cry of pain – it's demented anger!

Von Wolfenbüttel lowers his blade, clutches his right shoulder, draws back his hand and stares at the blood. His head snaps around. He looks at me, his face twisted in a rage more explosive then a detonated gunpowder keg.

God help me!

I may have saved Armand, but I don't like my chance of surviving the next few seconds.

CHAPTER THIRTEEN

Von Wolfenbüttel comes at me with the fury of a charging bear, practically snorting steam through his nostrils, blood hammering in his temple, his blade slashing wildly. If ever there was a time for divine intervention, it would be right now. But no angel miraculously materialises to repel von Wolfenbüttel's attack, and for the second time today I'm left to fend for myself.

I'm almost bowled over by von Wolfenbüttel's charge. I barely manage to side-step his assault and prepare a defensive stance. Then he's on top of me like a thunderstorm, his blade delivering a barrage of lightning bolts. Terrified, I cower in fear and give ground, keeping my guard up in a desperate attempt to stay alive. I give ground so rapidly that I'm sure it's the only thing keeping me alive, for von Wolfenbüttel cannot get close enough to deliver a killing blow. I just pray that Armand will soon come to his senses and save me. Otherwise, it will only be a matter of time before my luck runs out and I end up skewered on the end of von Wolfenbüttel's rapier.

Fortunately, my pistol shot managed to cripple von Wolfenbüttel, putting his right arm – his sword-arm – out of action. He's now wielding his blade in his left hand, moving with far less confidence. His attack is still relentless and impossibly strong, raining blows upon me like a blacksmith hammering a bar of hot iron into shape.

All I can hear is the squeal of our blades and the shuffle of our feet across the flagstone floor of the courtyard. Whereas von Wolfenbüttel is evidently experienced in the art of swordplay and comes after me in a traversing dance of death, I am simply fighting to stay alive. Oddly, I find myself recalling Armand's earlier comment that a sword hums a song when it enters combat. I wish the song made by von Wolfenbüttel's blade would hurry up and end. Then I could pass von Wolfenbüttel off to another dancing partner. As Armand is still struggling to gain his feet, however, it looks as though I'm going to have to see this dance out.

But this is starting to take its toll on my sword hand. My blade is vibrating fiercely, making my hand numb. I feel like discarding my blade and dunking my hand into a bucket of chilled water. But there's no such luxury here. Not when I'm fighting for my life. And so my blade works overtime, transformed into a blur of silver, trying desperately to parry von Wolfenbüttel's storm of steel. If I can make it to the other side of the keep, Robert, positioned above us in the tower, will be able to get a clear shot at him. Though any hope of achieving that goal is lost when I'm forced back through the hole in the wall.

I have barely entered the room, the floor of which is littered with smoking chunks of stone torn from the walls and ceiling by the exploding bomb, when I trip over some rubble and lose my footing. I fall backwards, my eyes wide with terror, as I watch von Wolfenbüttel tear after me, his blade drawn back in preparation to skewer me where I lie. Driven by fear, I scramble desperately across the floor, narrowly avoiding his blade, making it back to the room's doorway. I barely have time to climb to my feet before von Wolfenbüttel swings wildly at my head. I duck instinctively, and the blade, which whizzes through the air only an inch above my head, hits the wall at full force.

I scramble back into the central corridor, just as I see a massive chunk of rock, dislodged by the impact of von Wolfenbüttel's blade, fall from the doorway's lintel. But von Wolfenbüttel, standing directly beneath the lintel, cannot see it coming, and the first knowledge he has of the falling rock is when it crashes down onto his head. There's a sickening crack, and he slumps to his knees, his features contorted in pain. But the impact, which would have cracked the skull or snapped the neck of a lesser man, only serves to infuriate von Wolfenbüttel. His eyes blazing with savage fury, and blood streaming from the open wound on the top of his head, he pushes himself to his feet and staggers after me.

I move down the corridor, somehow managing to hold my ground, my blade a whirr of slashing silver. Just when I think I can't hold out much longer, and I start to wonder what has become of my remaining companions – who I thought would have come to my aid by now, the last I saw of them being when they hastened into the room on the opposite side of the corridor – von Wolfenbüttel's storm starts to abate. Can it be that he's starting to tire? There's a trail of blood dripping freely down the side of his head, and the pistol wound he received earlier is sapping his strength. I only have to withstand a few more savage lunges before he pauses, steps back, breathes heavily, and holds his blade low.

My confidence gaining each second, and the call of my father's blood spurring me onward, I shuffle forward and engage von Wolfenbüttel in a new dance. However, this time I lead, pressing the attack, testing how much energy he has left. But I move cautiously. He's tricked me once before into committing an attack that left me exposed and vulnerable, so I'm wary that his fatigue may be feigned.

Taking Armand's previous advice, I decide it's time to see if I can orchestrate a symphony of death. But whilst I have the will, I lack the skill, and my symphony of death degenerates into a hotchpotch of desperate thrusts followed by panicked gambles at defence against von Wolfenbüttel's counter-attacks. I'm just lucky that my opponent is not only exhausted and badly wounded, but his sword-arm has been incapacitated. Otherwise, I fear I would have been killed in the opening second of this fight.

But there's no need to hurry my attack, for time is on my side. Quite remarkably, the only wound I have sustained from von Wolfenbüttel has been the slash across my shoulder. Although the wound is sore, it is bearable, and it's certainly not taking as much of a toll on me as the wounds sustained by von Wolfenbüttel. Armand has finally regained his feet, collected his blades and staggered into the corridor. Still, he won't be coming to my aid just yet. He's collapsed against the wall, and only seems vaguely aware of his surroundings.

Taking a deep breath, I try to relax my breathing and recall some of the attacks I had studied in Salvator Fabris's treatise on the art of swordplay. There was an attack in the second chapter that I had once practised for an entire week. Deciding to see if it will work in practice, I take two steps forward, feign to thrust at von Wolfenbüttel's torso and, at the last moment, flick my wrist up, redirecting my blade at his face.

Von Wolfenbüttel shuffles back and manages to parry the attack. But only just. Before he has time to regain his composure, I lunge forward with a linear thrust directed at his right thigh. Caught by surprise, von Wolfenbüttel sweeps his blade wide across his body. It's a desperate attempt to block my attack. And it fails.

I give a triumphant cry as my rapier bites deep into its target, delivering a deep, crippling wound. I'm sure that such a wound would normally mark the end of a duel, the certain incapacitation of its recipient. Before I can withdraw my blade, von Wolfenbüttel does the *impossible*: he snatches the blade of my rapier with his gloved hand.

A vicious tug of war develops. My blade slices through the leather glove, biting deep into von Wolfenbüttel's fingers. But he holds fast, his fingers locked around my rapier like a vice. I feel as though I'm one of King Arthur's contenders, trying to draw Excalibur from the stone.

The next instant, he bites his bottom lip in pain and yanks back his right foot, dislodging me from my feet, and drawing me straight into his chest. Arms like iron lock around me. I try to wrestle free, but it's useless. I might as well be trying to break through prison cell bars.

As if things couldn't get any worse, one of von Wolfenbüttel's hands clamps around my neck and starts to squeeze the life out of me. In desperation, I grab my rapier – still impaled in his thigh – and drive it deeper into his leg. His body shudders in pain, but he doesn't release his grip. If anything, he seems to squeeze even harder

The pain is unbearable! I fear my neck is going to snap. Everything's starting to go blurry and I can't breathe. If one of my companions doesn't come to my rescue this very instant I'm sure I'll be dead within the next few heartbeats. But none of the Hexenjäger appear, and with what I'm sure is my dying breath, I reach for the remaining pistol tucked into my belt, and – *BLAM!* – discharge it straight into von Wolfenbüttel's chest.

Von Wolfenbüttel releases his grip instantly. I slump to the floor, gulping air like a fish out of water. And it's then, through tear-filled eyes, I see von Wolfenbüttel and shake my head in disbelief.

Impossible! He's still standing.

With a resolve I never knew I had, I reach out, extracting my rapier from von Wolfenbüttel's thigh. I then clamber to my feet.

'You cannot be human!' I cry.

In response, von Wolfenbüttel, his features still twisted in rage, lets a fist – the size of a shoulder of ham – fly at my face.

That's not exactly the reply I was expecting. I pull back my head at the last moment, turning a direct hit into a glancing blow. Still, it's enough to knock me off my feet. It feels as if my nose has been spread an extra two inches across my face.

I scramble back across the floor, holding my rapier before me in a futile attempt at defence. But von

Wolfenbüttel doesn't pursue his attack. Instead, he staggers back, one hand clutching his chest; the other still gripping his blade. He then steadies himself, braces himself against the corridor wall and stares at me through death-glazed eyes.

He's an absolute mess. His tabard is drenched in blood, his features twisted in pain, and he can barely lift his sword. I'm amazed that he can muster the strength to stand.

I regain my feet. But there's no point in carrying on with this fight. Von Wolfenbüttel doesn't even stir. He looks as though he's going to drop dead at any moment. I lower my blade, signifying the fight is over.

Now I can hear sounds of combat coming from within the keep – from the floor directly above me, to be precise. I can clearly identify Lieutenant Blodklutt barking commands, and the distinct twang and squeal of steel on steel. My remaining companions must have located Leopold von Wolfenbüttel and the Holy Spirit.

This is all too much. I've been nearly scratched to death by a witch, had a bomb explode near me, battled the most feared man in Europe, been slashed across the shoulder, strangled, and – finally – punched. The last thing I feel like doing is tearing into another fray. Can't I just call it a day and sheathe my blade? Find the nearest inn and fall asleep in a hot bath? I don't think my fellow companions would begrudge me that simple pleasure. I've done more than my fair share of fighting today.

Yet my companions may be in danger. I'm not sure how much assistance I'll be able to offer them, but I can't just wait here, listening to the sounds of combat, skulking like some coward in the shadows.

I salute von Wolfenbüttel with my blade and move to walk past him. Too tired to even clutch his wounds, and slumped against the wall, he looks as if he is at death's door. But a restraining hand seizes my shoulder.

Armand steps past me. 'You're a young man full of surprises, Jakob,' he says, staring at von Wolfenbüttel and wiping a sleeve across his shattered mouth. 'Not only have you slain three witches today, but you have defeated one of the most feared killers in the Holy Roman Empire. I am in debt to you. It looks as if you saved my life. But this fight isn't over yet. It's best if you leave the final stroke to me.'

Realising he intends to kill von Wolfenbüttel – who is struggling to find the energy to stand, let alone raise his sword in defence – I shake my head and grab Armand. 'For the love of God, Armand, have some mercy. Can't you see the man is dying? This fight is finished.'

Armand pulls away from me, looks at me apologetically. 'You should know that war is a bloody affair. And in this case, I cannot exercise mercy. He has killed more men than you could ever imagine. To let him walk from here would be a grave mistake. I like this no more than you do, but you must learn that God and priests deal with mercy. We deal with death.'

I realise that Armand and I are a world apart. I could never bring myself to kill an injured person, even an enemy who had only moments before been trying to take my own life. There are some fundamental qualities – such as compassion and mercy – that lie deep in my heart, and I will not compromise them. Once that line is crossed, I believe I would lose the qualities that make me human, and make me no better than an animal. I would have taken my first steps on the bloody path of a cold-blooded killer. And I am not prepared to take those steps.

'I'm sorry, but I can't allow you to do this,' I say, and place myself between Armand and von Wolfenbüttel. 'I won't allow you to kill an injured man.'

'Please, Jakob, step aside. Don't make this any harder than it already is.'

'Armand, please!' I say imploringly, and hold Armand with my eyes. 'This man is already at death's door. He is no longer a threat to us. There has been too much killing today. If there is going to be any good to come out of this mission, let it be this one act of mercy. Please. You told me before that you hoped to achieve your soul's salvation by following a path of righteousness. Then let this be your first step.'

Armand looks at me for some time before his eyes soften in acquiescence. 'I may live to regret this decision,' he says reluctantly and sheathes his blades. 'But you are right – there has been a lot of bloodshed this day. Perhaps some good will come from sparing this man's life.'

I pat Armand on the shoulder and smile gratefully, thankful that he heeded my appeal for clemency.

A pistol shot shatters the stillness from behind me.

What?

Armand is hit! He spins like a top before he slams – headfirst – into the corridor wall. There's a sickening crack, like a watermelon being thrown against a brick wall. Then he slumps to the floor.

Horrified, I snap around, just in time to see the guard of a rapier crash into my jaw, knocking me senseless to the ground.

⫶CHAPTER⫶ FOURTEEN

A blinding pain in my shoulder draws me back to consciousness.

I stir, raise myself onto an elbow and take in my surroundings. I'm lying on a rubble-strewn floor in an unfamiliar room – an abandoned banquet hall, by the look of it. There's a hearth in the far corner, and a large central table, surrounded by over two dozen chairs, dominates the room. Paintings, mostly portraits, adorn the walls. There must be over fifty of them. Some look hundreds of years old, the oil cracked and peeling. They are all of women, clad in rags stained yellow with age, and their crooked noses and evil eyes make my skin crawl.

To my surprise, my weapons are stacked in a pile by my side. All of my wounds have been bandaged and a sweet-smelling salve has been applied to my bruised jaw. In spite of this, my body is riddled with aches and pains, and I lay there for a while, trying to work out what has happened. I can recall the fight with von Wolfenbüttel and my argument with Armand. A cold shudder runs down my spine as I recall a pistol being fired, hitting Armand, and then a rapier being smashed into my jaw. For some strange reason, I cannot remove the image of a wolf from my mind. But I have no recollection as to how I ended up in this room. I must have been carried here when I was unconscious.

There are voices over to my right, raised in argument. Someone's blaspheming loudly, savagely. A pack of rabid dogs fighting over a bone are more cordial.

I crane my head around, my eyes locking instantly on a body near the hearth, lying in a pool of blood. I can't see the face, but the clothing reveals that it's not one of our order. I can only assume that it must be one of the Brotherhood of the Cross.

Then I find my companions, and blink back against the impossibility of what I see. Are my eyes deceiving me? Is this some fatigue-induced illusion? It must be. Why else would Lieutenant Blodklutt have von Frankenthal, Bethlen and Armand – who I can't believe is still alive – bailed up against a wall?

And at gunpoint!

I climb to my feet. A wave of dizziness overcomes me, and I'm forced to wait several seconds before the reeling sensation subsides. Having equipped my weapons, I make my way over to the Lieutenant, who turns and looks at me. He offers no welcoming smile to see me up on my feet again, just a cold stare. His features are set in a determined scowl, as if he has a grim task ahead of him.

I point at the body by the hearth. 'Who's that? What's going on?'

'Leopold von Wolfenbüttel,' he says dismissively, as if he has more pressing concerns to deal with. And, by the looks of it, he does. 'Here,' he adds, and tosses me a rope. 'I want them bound.'

'I won't be tied up like some stuck pig!' von Frankenthal roars at Lieutenant Blodklutt. 'Lower that blasted weapon!'

Von Frankenthal is standing against the wall along with Armand and Bethlen. Their hands are raised above their heads, and their weapons lie out of reach in a bundle on the central table. I've never seen von Frankenthal so furious. I just hope he doesn't lose complete control of his temper.

Lieutenant Blodklutt aims his pistol directly at him. 'You move an inch and I'll shoot! And you know I'll do it.'

I shake my head in confusion, struggling to comprehend what's happening. 'Let's just all calm down. Can someone please tell me what's going on?'

My words fall on deaf ears. If Blodklutt is staring daggers, von Frankenthal is staring a double-handed broadsword. It's going to take more than a simple plea to defuse this situation.

'You had better make sure you tie me up well,' von Frankenthal rumbles at me. 'Because the second I'm free there's going to be a bloodbath!'

The menace in his voice is enough to make my hands tremble, and I look across at Blodklutt, afraid of what to do. But the Lieutenant doesn't take his eyes off von Frankenthal. He gestures towards the Hexenjäger with his pistol.

'Go ahead,' he instructs me. 'Tie them up.'

I take a hesitant step forward, but then stop. What am I to do? I feel caught in the middle. I don't want to disobey a direct order from a senior member of the Hexenjäger, but I cannot bring myself to bind my companions, particularly Armand, who has become a friend and mentor. And, mixed loyalties aside, I'd rather not get on von Frankenthal's bad side.

'What about him?' Bethlen blurts out, obviously trying to save his own skin, and points at me. 'He's the one you're after. I know he is. I wouldn't trust him as far as I can shoot.'

I look at Bethlen and shake my head in disgust. I have no idea what's going on, but I'm sure he'd betray his own mother if it meant saving his own skin.

'Robert and Jakob are the only people on this mission who I know I can trust,' Blodklutt says. 'Now, not another word from you.'

'But . . .'

The Lieutenant directs his pistol at Bethlen. 'I said not another word. Now, Jakob, tie them.'

I cross reluctantly over to my companions and start to bind Bethlen's hands behind his back. He struggles at first and pushes his shoulder into my chest, forcing me back several steps. Bethlen stops struggling once the Lieutenant levels his pistol at him, allowing me to finish binding his arms.

'You'll pay for this, whelp!' he says, glaring at me.

Ignoring the comment, I move over to Armand. 'I'm glad to see you,' I whisper in his ear. 'I thought you were dead.'

'It's going to take more than a graze from a pistol ball to kill me,' he whispers back.

My mind flashes back to the corridor and the final moments of the encounter with von Wolfenbüttel. I remember the pistol shot hitting Armand, spinning him like a top and slamming him headfirst into the wall. But whereas I had thought that the shot had killed him, the ball must have only grazed his left shoulder. That would account for the fresh bandage applied there. It doesn't, however, solve the mystery as to who attacked us in the corridor. It had to have been the Holy Spirit. With Leopold lying dead in this room, who else could it have been? Maybe Lieutenant Blodklutt and the others might be able to shed some light on the matter. But I don't think right now is the best moment to raise the issue. It's best if I first find out what's happening.

'What's going on?' I whisper, my hat tilted low so that the Lieutenant can't see my lips move.

'I don't know,' Armand returns, his hat likewise tilted, his eyes narrowed suspiciously. 'But this isn't good. It's best if you just go along with Blodklutt for the moment. He thinks he can trust you. I hope you know who your friends are here.'

'Don't worry about that,' I say, ensuring that Armand's hands are bound loosely, making for an easy escape if need be.

'So what do you intend to do with us now?' von Frankenthal asks, his voice a rumble of barely controlled rage.

'Find out the truth,' Lieutenant Blodklutt returns.

'The truth? Concerning what?' Armand asks, baffled.

'Over the course of the past year, many of our order have met with peril,' the Lieutenant explains. 'What should have been relatively easy missions have resulted in the death of some of our most seasoned fighters. When seven Hexenjäger failed to return from a simple reconnaissance mission to a graveyard on the outskirts of Wittenberg last April, we started to get suspicious. Captain Faust and I were sent to the town to investigate the matter. But the Hexenjäger didn't even make it to their destination. We found their bodies in shallow graves by the roadside. We exhumed them, and discovered that several had died by single pistol shots to the forehead. Upon further investigation, we found that they had been killed with silver pistol balls – engraved with crucifixes.'

121

What? Kurt von Wolfenbüttel? A cold chill settles into my bones and makes the hair on my arms stand on end.

'We also learned that the Brotherhood of the Cross had eliminated the other Hexenjäger,' Lieutenant Blodklutt continues. 'They were targeting our order. It was obvious that they were being informed of our movements. And so we started to look *within* the Hexenjäger for the leak.

'Captain Faust had been working in secret for some time; not searching for the Trumpet of Jericho, but spying on our order. He's been watching your movements, studying who entered and left Burg Grimmheim, trying to find out how information was being passed onto the Brotherhood. It didn't take him long to learn that there was a spy within our ranks.' The Lieutenant pauses for effect and studies the faces of the three men held at gunpoint, analysing their reactions. 'This entire mission was designed to catch that spy. It's nothing more than a mole hunt.'

I'm about to start tying von Frankenthal, but I stop. Did I just hear that right? A mole hunt? And a spy within the Hexenjäger! This is hard to digest. We're wearing expressions on our faces as though we've just witnessed the Resurrection.

'So what of the trumpet? And what of the Blood Countess?' I blurt out.

Blodklutt's eyes are locked on the three suspects. 'I'm sure the trumpet exists,' he says. 'But we're not going to find it. We concocted the story of the labyrinth and trumpet to ensure that we could lure the Brotherhood here. They would not be able to resist such bait. And as for the Countess – well, she exists. And I intend to deal with her once we resolve this issue.'

Von Frankenthal has calmed down now, but he's certainly not happy with Blodklutt's news. He shakes his head in bewilderment. 'What makes you so sure that the spy is one of us?'

'Captain Faust narrowed his investigation to four suspects,' the Lieutenant explains. 'You three, and Klaus. But since Klaus was killed by the Brotherhood, we can eliminate him from the list. They would not risk killing their own spy. And although you assisted me in fighting Leopold, your blade never drew his blood. Nor did Bethlen's, for that matter. It was my blade *alone* that slew him. I can personally vouch for Robert, and Jakob has only been with us for one week.

'We know for a fact that the spy infiltrated the Hexenjäger over a year ago, corresponding with the time that you three joined our order.' The Lieutenant pauses as he studies the reactions of the witch hunters from behind the barrel of his pistol. 'It also seemed too coincidental that the three of you were present in the Grand Hexenjäger's office, when the ill-fated mission to the graveyard in Wittenberg had been assigned. Along with Klaus, you were all part of the initial team, but had to be reassigned to other missions later that evening. You were the only ones who knew the exact route the Hexenjäger were going to take. Although you were all reassigned to different missions, you would have had time to pass a message on to the Brotherhood of the Cross. And there have been other instances where you have been reassigned, only for the original missions to end in peril.' He pauses, his steel-grey eyes narrowing menacingly. 'Meaning that one of you is the spy. And we aren't leaving this room until I work out who it is.'

Shocked, I step warily away from my companions. One of them is a spy for the Brotherhood of the Cross. But who? I have no reason whatsoever to suspect von Frankenthal. Apart from the incident with Gerhard, I actually don't know much about the man. And I'd hate to think that it would be Armand. He has, however, led an immoral past. Could it be that his penance and desire to start life anew are simply feigned? Has he been hired by the Brotherhood to infiltrate the Hexenjäger and pass on information vital to the destruction of the order? The lure of gold can turn many a man's heart, even upright and righteous men who do not have shadowy pasts.

If the spy is not von Frankenthal or Armand, then it must be Bethlen. He has confessed to rising to his position in life through cunning and brawn. He comes across as somewhat of an opportunist, and I don't feel there is much loyalty in his heart to any cause. He's the sort of person who could be easily swayed by the promise of gold. Furthermore, I recall the feigned surprise in his voice when we first discovered that someone else was inside the castle.

Had he known all along that the Brotherhood of the Cross were inside Schloss Kriegsberg? Could he be the one who informed them of our actions?

'You're taking one hell of a risk tying us up,' Armand says, rolling his wounded shoulder, trying to make himself more comfortable. 'If what you are saying is correct, then two of us are innocent. And there are still witches and the Countess hiding somewhere within these walls, not to mention the Holy Spirit and Kurt von Wolfenbüttel. I don't even want to think about what will happen if they suddenly decide to converge on this room. We won't be much help to you all tied up. It will be up to you and Jakob.'

Now that's a very valid point. I suddenly feel vulnerable, and cast an uneasy eye around the room, half expecting a swarm of crones to burst in on us. I don't know how long Lieutenant Blodklutt and I would last against them.

It's also only now I become aware that I've been so intent on listening to the Lieutenant that I haven't bound von Frankenthal's hands. I don't think I will, either. If he is the spy, then Blodklutt can take care of him with his pistol. But if he isn't the spy, I'd hate to have tied up von Frankenthal and have the witches appear.

A striking thought makes my brow crease in confusion. Did Armand say that von Wolfenbüttel is still hiding somewhere within the keep? How is that possible? Not unless the man is descended from Lazarus. The man was at death's door when I last saw him.

'Kurt von Wolfenbüttel?' I question. 'He could barely stand. How can he still be alive?'

Armand shakes his head. 'I don't know. But apparently he is.'

'That's impossible. Where's your evidence?'

Armand gestures with his head towards the Lieutenant. 'Ask him.'

'I found you and Armand lying unconscious in the corridor,' Blodklutt explains. 'I conducted a quick search of the ground floor of the keep – there was no sign of Kurt. Until we find his body we had best consider him alive and dangerous.'

'They don't call him the man who can't be killed for nothing,' Armand adds. 'But back to more pressing concerns, how are you going to find out who the spy is? Brand us with hot irons? Look, I just want this matter resolved as quickly as possible.'

I don't think Lieutenant Blodklutt's going to rush this. From what I've seen, he's a man of patience. It wouldn't surprise me if some of us start balding before we exit this hall.

'We'll take as long as it takes,' he says, his voice cold. Even an executioner's sneer has more compassion.

Armand lowers his head in resignation. He looks up again, as if to say something, but he catches himself and cranes his head forward. His eyes narrow, and he stares at me, hard.

'That mark on your face,' he says, and gestures with his eyes towards my left cheek. 'How did you get it?'

I touch my wounded jaw. 'Compliments of the man who shot you. He smashed his rapier into my face. But it all happened so fast that I never got to see who it was.'

'I think I've just worked that out,' Armand says.

'What?'

'Come here. Show me your face. I just need to see the mark.'

I take three hesitant steps forward, allowing Armand to study the bruise. His eyes flash suddenly in recognition.

'Look out the window, Jakob,' he instructs. 'Quickly. Tell me what you see.'

'Wait. What are you up to?' Blodklutt is suspicious, his pistol aimed at Armand.

'Just let Jakob tell you what he sees in the courtyard.' There's an urgency in Armand's voice, as if his life depends on it. 'Now. Quickly!'

Blodklutt nods, and I move over to a window to look out over the inner courtyard. 'I see the buildings,' I say. 'The rubble from the bomb. Captain Faust's body.'

Then I realise what I'm *supposed* to see. But it's not there.

The hairs almost shoot out of my skin. I turn and look at my companions.

'There's no sign of Klaus!'

CHAPTER FIFTEEN

'You can't see Klaus, because he never died,' Armand warns.

I turn from the window and stare at Armand, struggling to comprehend this revelation.

'But that can't be possible. I saw him. He was dead!' I say, the words blurting out of my mouth like water gushing through a burst dike. 'He never survived the grenade blast. I saw the blood . . . his eyes.'

Armand shakes his head. 'You thought he was dead. But he was only *playing* dead. It was all staged. The mark on your jaw reveals as much. You can't see it, but it has developed into a unique bruise – a *wolf's head*, to be precise; the exact same emblem that appears on the guard of Klaus's rapier.' He pauses, looks across at Lieutenant Blodklutt. 'It's no great mystery as to who shot me and punched Jakob unconscious. And it's no great mystery as to who your spy is.'

The Lieutenant strides over to the window, checks for himself. He slams a clenched fist on the sill in frustration. He then comes over to me, grabs me by the chin, tilts my head and examines the mark on my jaw. The Lieutenant steps back, stunned. He's wearing an expression like someone who's just discovered they've been cheated out of their inheritance by some unknown relative.

Klaus. A spy! In league with the Brotherhood of the Cross.

This is all too much. I shake my head in disbelief. At least now I have an answer as to why, when I first woke in this room and tried to recall the events that had transpired in the corridor, I could not shake the image of a wolf from my mind. The wolf's head, carved into the guard of Klaus's rapier, was the last thing I had seen before being knocked unconscious.

'Untie them,' Lieutenant Blodklutt instructs me, trying to salvage what dignity he can from the situation.

I've only taken one step, when I hear the distinct click of a pistol being cocked.

'You'll stay where you are. And you'll drop those weapons.'

I freeze in my tracks. I never thought I'd hear *that* voice again. Only this time, it sounds distinctly different, laced with malice.

I turn slowly and look towards the single doorway leading into the hall, where a figure emerges from the shadows. I don't even have to see the man's face to know that it's Klaus Grimmelshausen.

An uneasy silence. The tension's so great you can practically see beads of sweat form in the air.

'Your weapons – drop them. Now!'

Lieutenant Blodklutt and I do as instructed. I start with my rapier, then my pistols and carbine. I place them on the ground, slowly, almost mechanically. I don't want to make any hasty movements and give Klaus an excuse to discharge his pistol at me.

'Now step back. Stop. That's enough. Put your hands on your head.'

Again, we do as ordered. We're not exactly in a position to do anything other than comply with his demands. Klaus has already shot Armand. I'm sure his next shot won't just wound someone in the shoulder. It will more likely send one of us straight to a grave.

'I've dreamed of this moment for some time,' Klaus says. 'But I never thought it was going to be this sweet. How ironic it is that you should learn of my deception only at the very moment I catch you at gunpoint.'

'But why?' Armand asks. 'How could you betray us?'

'Don't look so shocked. This has been planned for over a year now.'

Von Frankenthal shakes his head in disgust. 'So how much are they paying you? It must be a lot to make you turn traitor; to turn on the very order you have vowed to defend – to those who have treated you as a brother.'

'Don't talk to me of *brotherhood*. You who have so little understanding of what the term means.' Klaus spits the words out as if he has bile in his mouth. 'And don't you dare accuse me of being a traitor. I've remained true to my calling for the past year, enduring the blasphemous actions of your order. I was never part of your order. I was sent to infiltrate the Hexenjäger – to oversee its destruction.'

Klaus snickers, seeing our foreheads crease in confusion. 'Be careful who you call a traitor, for the only traitors in this room are the Habsburg scum who have betrayed God's law. You are abominations in the eyes of our Lord. You are not even fit to walk this world. And I intend to set things right.'

'You're no better than those who hired you,' I return, the feeling of betrayal overwhelming. 'You're no better than the Brotherhood of the Cross.'

'You still don't understand, do you?' Klaus returns. 'I *am* one of the Brotherhood of the Cross. I am the Holy Spirit.'

What? We stare dumbfounded at Klaus, struggling to comprehend this revelation. Then there's a shuffle from someone behind me. Klaus's pistol locks on the person faster than you can blink.

'Don't be a fool, Christian!' Klaus warns, his voice dripping with venom. 'But enough talk. Time to end this. Vengeance shall be mine.'

He steps into the room, moves over to the hearth where Leopold von Wolfenbüttel lies. He kneels down and places a finger on Leopold's neck, searching for a pulse. Finding none, he rises to his feet again. All the while his eyes are locked on us.

Maybe it's just that my perception of him has changed, but his eyes seem different. Perhaps it's a trick played by the shadows, but I'm certain his eyes have changed from light blue to jet black. All that remains is pure hatred ... and an unquenchable thirst for revenge.

This is not the man I knew. We are now staring face to face with the deadliest member of the Brotherhood of the Cross. And he intends to kill us all. I still can't believe this is happening. I was grieving the man's presumed death earlier today, and now I'm staring down the barrel of his pistol.

But we don't have time to ponder how we've been fooled. We have to act fast. We might only have seconds before Klaus launches upon us. I pity Bethlen, though. With his hands bound, he doesn't stand a chance. Klaus will tear into him like one of Hell's furies. But as desperate as our situation is, we still have some cards hidden up our sleeves.

Firstly, Klaus has only one pistol, meaning he gets only one shot at us. Even if he shoots one of us, he will have to face the rest of us with his blade. That won't be an easy task, particularly when he has to face Lieutenant Blodklutt and Armand.

Secondly, von Frankenthal's hands are not bound, and Armand will be able to break free with minimal effort. As far as Klaus knows, both men's wrists are tied, giving both von Frankenthal and Armand a vital element of surprise.

Thirdly, we have Robert outside, scanning the windows on the eastern side of the keep with his rifle. And, finally, I still have two weapons – my daggers – tucked into the folds of my boots. Although I've never thrown a dagger before, I'm sure that my attempt would at least momentarily distract Klaus, possibly granting my companions time to arm themselves.

And so the waiting game begins to see who will make the first move. Hell is about to break loose.

CHAPTER SIXTEEN

The standoff is unbearable. Seconds drag by so slowly it's like watching a wound fester.

Sweat starts to drip down my back and bead on my forehead. But I dare not wipe a sleeve against my brow. That simple move could be the match that ignites the powder keg and sends the room into chaos.

I catch Lieutenant Blodklutt in the corner of my eye. He looks as taut as an over-tightened violin string, his fingers twitching in nervous anticipation. But he knows that if he makes the first move he may become the target of Klaus's pistol.

We all know this. And so we wait to see what Klaus does.

It's at this critical point that Armand makes a last-ditch effort at diplomacy. He stands about as much a chance of succeeding in this as a highwayman who's trying to sweet-talk his way out of a hangman's noose. Still, I have to admire his spirit.

'Klaus, my dear friend, we are all gentlemen here,' he says. 'Surely this can be resolved in some other fashion. Please, lower your pistol. Let our blades slumber in their scabbards. They have worked hard today. Let them enjoy their sleep.'

'Be silent, French fop!'

Armand takes the rebuke graciously. He doesn't even flinch. There's too much at stake here.

'Come now. That's hardly conducive to resolving this slight hiccup.' Armand's even so bold as to take a step forward.

It's the last step he'll ever take. Not unless he can dodge pistol balls. For Klaus's finger tightens on the trigger.

'Armand! No!' I call out, fearing he will be shot. I squint my eyes in anticipation of the pistol's report, and I'm about to reach for one of the daggers concealed in my boots, when we hear a sound that makes our skin crawl.

It starts as a low murmur, like a distant moan. Even Klaus stays his trigger-finger. He casts about the room, fearful of what new terror the keep holds in store for us.

The sound gathers in momentum, gets louder, develops into a horrific wail that would make the lamentations of tortured souls in Purgatory sound like angels singing. Then, as suddenly as it started, the noise stops, leaving a deathly stillness.

'What devilry is this?' Klaus whispers, looking about the room.

'I don't know,' Armand says. 'But may I suggest a truce. Whatever made that noise, we stand a better chance against it together.'

Klaus doesn't get a chance to respond. For no sooner have the words left Armand's mouth than the portraits along the walls come to life.

My heart practically freezes with fright. Dear God, protect my soul!

Like a vision from a nightmare, the women in the paintings come alive, peeling themselves from the cracked canvases. There are over fifty of them, corresponding with the number of paintings on the walls. They are clad in clothing more ragged than century-old, threadbare burial shrouds. Their faces are wrinkled nightmares of hate and malice, and they give bloodcurdling screams that would make even the Devil's skin crawl. They have eyes like drops of congealed blood, and their fingernails resemble rusted dagger blades, which they use to scale the walls and climb along the ceiling – upside down!

There's no introduction needed to know which one is Countess Gretchen Kraus. The most beautiful woman I've ever seen, she stands out like a diamond in a slush-bucket. She can't be any older than twenty years of age, her skin as smooth as porcelain, her raven-black hair hanging in long tresses.

Not bad, considering she was born *last century.*

Whilst I'm rooted to the spot in fear, Blodklutt doesn't waste a second. He's already collected his weapons and moved over to free the other Hexenjäger. Rather than ready his blade, however, he produces the *Malleus Maleficarum* – the Hammer of the Witches – from its case. He then orders the rest of us to retrieve our weapons and form a protective circle around him in the centre of the room.

Doing as instructed, we form a protective ring of steel around Blodklutt. That is, of course, all of us but Klaus. He hasn't moved and is cursing under his breath, staring with hatred at the witches.

'Whatever happens,' Armand calls out over the screeching mass of crones, 'do not let any get through to the Lieutenant. There are too many witches for us to deal with, and we are going to need the magic of the Hammer of the Witches if we are to survive. So *nothing* gets past us. If Blodklutt falls, we *all* die.' He points one of his sabres at the Holy Spirit. 'Klaus – we are in need of your blade. We need to put our differences aside for the moment. You must join us and fight the common enemy. Believe me, I like this no better than you do. But we have no other choice.'

Klaus glares at Armand, his eyes blazing with hatred. 'We get through this mess first,' he snarls, his lips curled in distaste, and pushes in beside me. 'Then I'll kill you all!'

Not comfortable in having to fight alongside a man who has vowed to kill us, I grip my rapier, assume a defensive stance, and press in close between Armand and Klaus. I wish I had a pistol readied, but I used both against Kurt von Wolfenbüttel. And I don't like my chances of getting them loaded right now.

The Countess's voice rises over the demonic cacophony of her coven.

'*Let's feast!*'

⚔CHAPTER
SEVENTEEN

The crones tear into us with a speed that leaves me gaping. Before I know what's happening, the witches are screaming around the room like harpies, their claws slashing wildly, slicing through us like razors. This is comparable to standing in the centre of a rag and dagger-laden tornado. In only a matter of seconds I'm bleeding from over a dozen fresh wounds. Fortunately they are not deep, but they are stinging like paper-cuts that have been doused in salt.

I strike back with my blade, but it's impossible to land a hit. By the time you can distinguish a crone amidst the screeching storm, she's disappeared into the whirl of movement. I feel as though I'm chasing shadows. I start slashing wildly, in the hope that one of the witches may end up skewering herself on my blade.

No sooner have I had the idea than – *slice*. There's an agonised scream as a witch impales herself on my rapier. I try to free my blade, but the crone isn't dead, my blade having only skewered the witch through the lower left-hand side of her torso. To my horror, she starts pulling herself along my rapier, her mouth wide open in preparation to set her rotted teeth into my flesh.

I move to give her a kick guaranteed to send her flying, but I'm distracted as something splatters on my hat. I snap my head up, dreading what I'm going to see, and look directly into the eyes of a witch, only *inches* from my face! She's salivating gobs of drool and hanging from the ceiling by her feet like some horribly mutated bat. A spider-web of blue veins ripples under the cadaver-white flesh of her face, and she has breath that would send a sewer rat gagging.

Before I have time to react, her hands shoot out. They latch onto my head, and she forces me to stare into her bloodshot eyes.

'Hello, Pretty,' she cackles, her voice sounding like a rusted coach wheel.

'Goodbye, Ugly!' I scream back, horrified.

Then, in a desperate act, I momentarily hold on to my rapier with only one hand, and reach down to my boots, producing a dagger. I thrust upwards, aiming at the witch's heart, intending to deliver a blow that will kill her instantly, and my ears are assailed by a bloodcurdling scream. The hag drops to the floor, writhing in pain, clutching the dagger buried in her chest, allowing me to turn and face the monstrosity that has now dragged itself along the length of my rapier.

I'm face to face with another crone. Veins writhe across her face like snakes. Her mouth is a gaping maw, spraying spittle. She pulls herself even closer in preparation to bite into me, revealing an eel-like, pus-infected tongue.

Aghast, I act instinctively, slamming a fist into the witch's face, knocking her off my blade. She scrambles across the floor, nursing her injuries. And I lunge forward, my blade aimed at her heart.

But then the crone starts muttering something in a language that sounds like a dog gnawing on a bone. Before I know what's happening, the muscles in my lower legs become unresponsive, beset by a numbing paralysis. The sensation shoots up my thighs, and within a matter of seconds I'm frozen stiff from the stomach down. I try desperately to move my legs, to break free from the invisible restraints of the witch's dark magic, but it's useless. It feels as if I have been buried from the navel down in hardened lime mortar.

The witch smiles maliciously, knowing that I'm at her mercy. She regains her feet and brandishes her dagger-like fingernails, taunting me. She licks her tongue across her lips, savouring her anticipated kill.

Perhaps the inscription on the blade of my rapier has safeguarded the upper half of my body from the witch's

141

spell. While I can still wield my sword, it's going to be impossible to mount an effective defence against her.

I have to try to break the spell. But I can't get close enough to the hag to strike at her with my rapier. My only other option is to try to gain the remaining dagger tucked in the fold of my left boot. If only I can reach it, I might be able to throw it at her. But it's impossible. With the lower half of my body frozen, I can't even reach a hand down far enough to find my boot.

Overwhelmed by the hopelessness of my situation, I cry out for help. A quick look around the room reveals that I can't rely upon my companions for assistance. Many of them are faring no better than I am.

Six yards or so off to my left, Bethlen has been dragged to the ground by three hags. He has one in a headlock, trapped under his left arm. But one of the remaining witches has her claws locked about his neck, squeezing with all her strength. It's the third hag, however, who's causing Bethlen the real problem. She's grabbed him by the hair, and is pulling so hard you'd think she's trying to pull a stump out of the ground. How she hasn't ripped Bethlen's scalp off is nothing short of a miracle.

Von Frankenthal is faring better than Bethlen. He's already killed two witches, dragged them screaming out of the air. He snapped the neck of one with his bare hands, and turned the second into a pincushion with his blade. But he's been wounded. His tabard and shirt have been torn open, revealing a savage cut across his chest. But the wound has only angered him, sent him into a rage. He looks as if he could harrow Hell.

In contrast, Klaus and Armand make the rest of us look like a pack of amateurs. Their blades are hissing streaks of silver, slicing through any witch foolish enough to come too close. Although I don't know how much longer Armand will be able to keep this up. He's nursing more injuries than an infirmary full of wounded soldiers.

Klaus has already vanquished three crones, their twisted bodies lying at his feet. He's moving with a relaxed fluidity, as though this is all second nature to him. His skill with a rapier almost defies comprehension, and I very much fear that, even if we manage to survive this encounter, we won't stand a chance against him. Perhaps the fight against the witches will remind Klaus and Lieutenant Blodklutt that we fight against a common evil, and that we should not allow our religious differences to make us enemies. I fear there's a greater chance of Hell converting to Christianity, however, before that will happen.

Neither Klaus nor Armand can come to my aid. They have taken positions on either side of Lieutenant Blodklutt, like sentinels guarding the entrance to the Holy of Holies. They are so focused on protecting him that neither is aware of my situation.

The Lieutenant's head is buried in the *Malleus Maleficarum*, mumbling phrases in some unknown language. I don't know if it's a figment of my imagination, but the leather-bound volume seems to be emitting a blue glow. However, it's not as if I'm in any position to wander over to have a closer look, particularly when the witch I'm facing has now closed to within striking range. And by the way she's brandishing her claws and staring at my throat, she intends to go straight for my jugular.

The hag's eyes lock on my rapier, the only thing keeping her at bay. She smiles maliciously, points at the blade with a bone-like finger, and starts to chant a different spell. The next instant, flames burst along the length of my sword. It's at this point – with the witch having broken her initial spell, which had paralysed me from the waist down – that I regain control of my feet.

I toss my blade aside as if it were an asp. But my rapier hasn't even touched the ground before the crone comes at me, as fast as a beggar diving on a coin, straight for my throat. I leap back, fumbling over a chair and losing my footing – just at the exact moment the witch flies past me. Her claws slash wildly at my throat. But her momentum carries her over my head, slamming her into the banquet table, knocking her senseless.

Knowing that I must capitalise on this opportunity, I scramble to my feet. I draw my remaining dagger and pounce onto the witch. One quick slash across her throat and it's all over.

Averting my eyes from the grizzly scene, I rise from

the crone's limp form and retrieve my rapier and daggers. Wiping the black blood from my trembling hands, I take some deep breaths and try to steady my nerves. I then stagger back to join the circle of steel guarding Lieutenant Blodklutt, struggling to comprehend how I've somehow managed to survive so far. I thought that last witch was going to kill me. It's fortunate that I tripped at the last moment. Otherwise I would be the one lying dead on the stone floor right now.

But this fight is far from over. I have to remain alert, prepared. Above all, I must not allow another witch to cast a spell on me. And yet I don't think anything could prepare me for what happens next.

Countess Gretchen Kraus pushes through the fray, emerges through the mass of hags like a rose sprouting through a dung-heap. There's a moment of silent anticipation. She stares at von Frankenthal, calls his name, forces him to return her stare. Then she whispers some obscure words, her voice like a breeze caressing silk curtains.

'No, Christian! Look away!' Armand's voice is piercingly high, as if an ammunitions wagon has just run over his toes, and he races over to von Frankenthal in an attempt to divert his attention from the Blood Countess.

But it's too late. For she has *bewitched* von Frankenthal with her eyes.

His body convulses, as if arsenic has been injected into his veins. He shakes as violently as a newborn calf on a freezing winter's night. He tries to fight against the evil forcing its way into his body. But it's too powerful, even for him.

It only takes a few seconds before he stops shaking. There's a moment of silence. Then he throws Armand aside as if he were a rag doll, turns and sets his eyes on me.

God help me!

Von Frankenthal has been possessed – transformed into the ultimate pawn of evil. He stares at me with such unbridled hatred you'd think I'd put his family to the sword.

My rapier suddenly feels useless. I don't even think a blunderbuss would be any help. What I need right now is an army of several thousand seasoned soldiers to protect me.

Why – out of all the people in the hall – did he have to target me? But it's no use complaining about that right now. As von Frankenthal lumbers towards me, my mind screams one word to my legs – *RUN!*

CHAPTER EIGHTEEN

Knowing that von Frankenthal is not a fast runner, I bolt from the room, hoping to outrun him. I never knew my legs could carry me so fast. It's just as well, for von Frankenthal's only a few yards behind me, a hulking mass of muscle and hatred, lumbering after me like the fall of Armageddon.

It doesn't take me long to develop a lead on him. Reaching the stairwell, I head upwards, taking the steps five at a time, my breathing coming in laboured gasps. The muscles in my legs scream for rest. But I dare not slow down, for to do so will mean that I will lose my lead, allowing von Frankenthal to gradually catch up to me. And that will mean certain death.

Von Frankenthal's the last person in the world I want to fight. Taking him on will be like trying to punch my way through a castle wall with my bare fists – an impossible task. And the situation's twice as bad now that he's been bewitched. I've heard that the possessed feel no pain. They continue fighting until they are literally cut to shreds. My only sure chance of survival is to kill the witch and break the spell. With von Frankenthal chasing after me, I don't like my chances of taking out the Blood Countess. I can only hope that my companions will take care of her.

Until then, all I can do is try to stay alive – focus on keeping out of von Frankenthal's reach. And so I scramble up the stairs, putting on a sudden spurt of energy, hoping to further increase my lead. I force my body to its limits and manage to gain a few extra yards on von Frankenthal, adding a brand to the fire of my hope. But fortune steps in and douses the fire, for the stairs come to an abrupt halt . . . in the form of a nail-studded door.

Damn!

I sprint up the stairs, only to find that the door is locked. I don't think I'd be able to barge it down with a battering ram, let alone with my bare shoulders in the few seconds I have to spare. My gaze races around the stairwell, look- ing for any possible means of escape. There's nothing but a window, set in the wall adjacent to the door, leading to nothing but blue sky and a stone gargoyle, over four yards long, attached to the keep wall some five yards off to the right of the window.

With von Frankenthal lumbering up the stairs, I sheathe

my rapier and commit to what could prove to be the most disastrous decision of my life – I dive out the window.

May the Lord protect me!

I never realised I had climbed to the very top of the keep – six storeys high! I sail through the air with the grace of a cow shot out of a trebuchet, my arms flailing as though I'm having a seizure.

Why did I ever do this? I'm going to die!

But then my fingers find purchase on something solid, allowing me get a firm grip with my hands. The gargoyle! I reached it. I can't believe my luck. I feel like screaming out in defiance of fate. Finally, something has gone my way.

As I pull myself up onto the gargoyle, I hear a blood-curdling roar from behind. I snap my head around, just in time to see von Frankenthal reach the window and dive out after me.

My blood runs cold, practically turns to ice, and I stare at von Frankenthal in shock. His massive form flies towards me, his eyes locked on mine the entire time, transfixing me with their burning hatred.

Then I come to my senses. *Move, move, move!* I scramble atop the gargoyle. But there's no time to brace myself for the impact. I have barely got my legs lifted to safety before von Frankenthal crashes into the structure.

WHOOMPH! He hits the gargoyle chest first, with the force of a galleon ramming into a wharf. There's a terrible retching sound as the wind explodes from his lungs. The rapier flies from his hand. The gargoyle reverberates with the force of the impact, but, fortunately, it doesn't break free from the wall.

With von Frankenthal momentarily winded, wrapped around the gargoyle, struggling to regain his breath, I seize the advantage. My first instinct is to kick him in the face – hard – with the heel of my boot. If I can force him to lose his grip, he will fall to the cobblestones below.

But I can't bring myself to do it. Not to one of my companions, even if he has been bewitched. I will only fight him as a last resort. And I wouldn't like my chances of surviving that encounter. He'd swat me aside, right before crushing my skull with his bare hands.

I shuffle back along the gargoyle, moving out of von Frankenthal's reach. I have to watch my balance, though. The gargoyle's no wider than two feet. There's little margin for error here. One false step and it's a hundred-foot drop to the courtyard for me.

I reach the wall of the keep, brace my back against it, and search for a means of escape. There's nowhere left to run. There's nothing beneath me but sheer wall. While there are gargoyles off to the left and right, they're over ten yards away. I'd never be able to reach them.

My only chance of flight lies in scaling the keep wall, all

ten feet of it. Then I can reach the crenellated battlement atop the keep. But I don't like my chance of doing that, not unless I can spring wings like Icarus.

Cornered, my hand flies instinctively to my rapier. I'm going to have to face von Frankenthal, and even though he's lost his blade, I'm sure I'll last no longer than a few seconds against him.

Trying not to panic, I take some deep breaths. I have to remain calm, try to keep my wits about me.

Just as I am starting to lose all hope, I see it: a fissure in the wall, directly in front of me, at a height of about four feet. It's only two inches wide and half a finger's-breadth thick – nothing more than an eye-slit in the stone. But it is large enough to wedge a dagger into, enabling me to create a foothold to scale the wall.

The next instant, I have a dagger in my hand and wedge it into the fissure. I stop, my heart missing a beat, for I sense a shadow looming behind me.

I spin around to find that von Frankenthal has regained his breath, pulled himself atop the gargoyle, and is now coming towards me. Fortunately, he's struggling to keep his balance, as nimble as a one-legged drunkard teetering atop a rolling wine barrel. He's inching closer nonetheless, his eyes still locked on mine.

Fighting back a rising wave of panic and fear, I focus on the wall. Hoisting a foot onto the dagger, I test my weight. Miraculously, it holds firm. With not a second to lose, I put my entire weight on it, plant my hands against the wall to stabilise myself, and push off, reaching for the top of the wall.

I reach it and start pulling myself up, dragging my torso over the wall. A second later and only my legs are left, dangling like bait before a shark. I'm almost there. I'm sure I'm going to make it. But the smile of victory disappears from my lips as a grip like a snapping bear-trap closes on my left ankle.

CHAPTER NINETEEN

C rying out in frustration, I snap my head around to stare down at von Frankenthal. He hasn't even stepped up onto my dagger. He's simply reached up and grabbed hold of me.

I try to kick free, but it's no use. Just as I think things can't get any worse, von Frankenthal gives a tremendous yank on my leg and tries to pull me down towards him.

NO!

Gritting my teeth, I cling to the wall. The muscles in my arms practically burst through my shirt with the effort. I feel like a rowboat facing an impossible struggle against the tremendous power of the Kraken. I'm almost torn from the wall. It's nothing short of a miracle my foot isn't dislocated. But somehow I manage to hold on.

After what seems to be an eternity, von Frankenthal

stops pulling. There's a reprieve as he readjusts his grip, prepares for a final assault on my leg; an assault that will rip me from the wall.

In desperation, I heave with all my strength. Heave until my face turns purple. Heave until the blood hammers in my temple. Heave until I fear my leg is about to snap off. Heave until . . . my leg slips *free* from the boot!

For a split second, time freezes. There's a look of utter disbelief on von Frankenthal's face. And then he topples backwards, staring at the boot in his hand.

Then time rushes back in, and I shoot free, propelled over the battlement, to lay sprawled on a parapet walk that runs around the inner perimeter of the roof. Without even bothering to see what has become of von Frankenthal, I scramble to my feet. Then I'm off.

I'm so exhausted it's a miracle I can still move. I've been pushed beyond my physical limits. Instinct alone propels me forward, cracking its whip across my back, squeezing the final drops of blood from my stamina stone.

It feels as though I'm in a dream, being chased by some fiendish horror. But as much as I will my legs to move, they're as responsive as wooden stumps. My wounded shoulder's screaming in pain. Each laboured breath's going down as easily as a mouthful of nails, and my tongue's sloshing about my mouth like a mop in a bucket. And yet the chase continues.

As far as I know, von Frankenthal might have

stumbled off the gargoyle and plummeted to his death. He might be splattered across the courtyard floor by now. Though I don't know that for certain. It's quite possible he's managed to regain his footing on the gargoyle, tossed aside my boot, and is preparing to scale the wall and give chase. Meaning I've only got a few seconds before his head rears over the battlement wall. Then the chase will begin all over again.

That's why I need to find a way off the roof – to disappear before von Frankenthal has a chance to spot me. If I can find a safe place to hide, then I can simply wait for one of my companions to kill the Countess; to remove the curse she placed upon von Frankenthal.

The parapet walk runs around the perimeter of the keep. On the inner side of the parapet – at a drop of over ten feet – lies a wooden roof. Its beams are so termite-infested that simply to breathe upon them would send them crumbling to dust. So I'm confined to the parapet walk.

I race around to the opposite side of the roof, searching for a means of escape. Finding none, I'm about to cry out in frustration when I see a trapdoor, some thirty yards off to my right, but with a mangonel parked on top of it.

Shaking my head in disbelief, I stagger over to the mangonel. Even though it's only a miniature catapult, it's over ten feet tall and must weigh over a tonne. This thing was built to last. It must be several hundred years old, but it looks as if it were built only yesterday.

There's no way I can access the trapdoor, as one of the mangonel's legs is parked directly on top of it. Unless I can harness the strength of an elephant, I severely doubt my chances of budging the mangonel even an inch.

And as if things cannot get any worse, it's then that I hear the roar – a roar that freezes my blood, inhuman in its bestial ferocity. I turn around, just in time to see von Frankenthal drag himself over the battlement.

⚔CHAPTER
TWENTY

Our eyes lock. There's a moment of silence as we stare at one another, waiting to see who will make the first move. It's not as if I'm going to be able to go far, though. All I'll be able to do is skirt around the parapet, ensuring I keep well away from von Frankenthal. It will then just come down to a question of endurance, to who tires first.

Von Frankenthal leaps from the battlement. He lands on the parapet on all fours, like some demonic panther. Then he springs to his feet and starts sprinting across the parapet.

And I'm off the next instant, moving in the opposite direction, charging around the mangonel. I've only taken three steps before I come to a sudden halt and stare down at the ground – at the coil of rope I have trodden upon.

I can't believe I didn't spot it earlier. I must have been so preoccupied with the trapdoor that I failed to see it.

The coil of rope must be over thirty yards in length. It's frayed in parts, but not beyond use. It looks as though it still has some strength in it. Enough strength, I hope, to support my weight.

It's the lifeline I need, the spark of hope that ignites the powder keg of my resolve. It brings an idea barging into my head that could see me escape from the roof.

But do I have time? Well, I'm not going to achieve anything just standing here procrastinating. It's time to move as if my life depends upon it, for von Frankenthal is only thirty yards away now, coming after me like Doomsday.

Without a second to spare, I snatch up the rope and loop it through one of the mangonel's legs. Having wrapped the ends of the rope around my hands, I then race forward, say a hasty prayer . . . and leap over the battlement.

I plummet down the side of the keep, the wind screaming in my ears and the stone wall rushing past me. Barely a second passes before – *TWANG* – there's a tremendous jolt as the rope runs its course. The rope bites into my flesh, slamming me into the wall of the keep. But I somehow manage to maintain my hold. I've fallen over a dozen yards. It's not exactly as far as I had hoped I would drop. By pure luck I've fallen far enough to bring me level with a window. It's no more than three yards off to my left.

Ignoring the pain in my hands, I plant my legs firmly against the wall. Grasping both lengths of rope in my right hand, I start to pull myself across to the left, reaching for the window. I have barely moved, however, when there's a powerful yank on the rope. My feet slip, and I'm dragged a good two yards up the wall.

I stare up in terror at von Frankenthal. He's straddling the battlements, pulling the rope, the muscles cording in his arms as he hoists me up.

Crying out in despair, I reach desperately across to the window, my fingers scrambling across the wall. But it's no use. It's beyond my reach.

Then there's another tug on the rope, lifting me higher, dragging me towards the battlements – taking me further away from the window; away from my only means of escape.

Realising I've only got one last hope, I take a deep breath, steeling myself for what I'm about to do. I then push off from the wall, swing out to the left, try to bring myself in line with the window . . . and let go of the rope.

I can't believe I'm doing this! This is arguably the most dangerous thing I've ever attempted in my entire life.

I'm falling fast. And I only get one shot at this. If I miss the window it's the courtyard floor for me. Certain death.

The wall flies past me in a blur of stone. Then a black hole appears – the window! I snap my hands out at just the right moment, catching hold of the window ledge, drawing my body in hard against the wall. The wind explodes from my chest, and the pain in my left shoulder is unbearable. But I manage to cling on.

I hang there for a moment, catching my breath, waiting for the pain to subside, amazed that I'm still alive. I've gambled with death too many times today. From here on, there's no more leaping out of windows, or jumping over castle walls, or letting go of a rope in the vain hope of catching hold of a window ledge. It's solid ground for me for the rest of my life.

But I'm not safe yet. Not until I climb through the window and get back inside the keep. As I start to pull myself up I become aware of movement over to my right.

I snap my head around to look at the rope. It's moving, jostling about as von Frankenthal starts to climb down the wall. He's lowering himself down the rope, coming after me.

No! I refuse to be caught. Not after all of this. And so, driven by fear alone, I scramble up the wall and haul myself up onto the window ledge. Propping myself up on

160

my elbows, I spare a second to stare into the room only to recoil in shock so that I nearly topple out of the window. For right in front of me is a witch whose blade-like finger-nails are set to sink into my skin.

⚔ CHAPTER ⚔
TWENTY-ONE

This cannot be happening! Everywhere I turn there's an obstacle in my way. But complaining about it isn't going to change the situation, and it certainly isn't going to make this witch disappear.

I'm not even free from von Frankenthal yet, and now I have this new terror – with teeth-like lumps of charcoal and a face riddled with scars and warts – to deal with. I'm hardly in any position to defend myself. I haven't even dragged my feet up yet. I fear I might fall to my death if I remove one of my hands from the ledge. But I don't have much of an option, for the crone's hands shoot out and start to claw at my face, trying to push me out the window.

Forced to defend myself, I brace my right elbow into the corner of the ledge, wedging myself in like a tick. I then try to fend off the attack with my left hand. But the witch is unrelenting, tearing at my face with savage fury.

I catch movement behind the witch, and pray that it isn't more crones. Stranded in the window, I won't stand a chance at fighting them off. I might as well let go right now, let myself fall to my death. At least then I won't have to endure the torture of having my face shredded.

All of a sudden I hear a voice, barking commands; a voice I would recognise anywhere, as foppish as a perfumed handkerchief. And it's coming from within the room.

Armand!

I try to crane my head around the witch to catch a glimpse of what lies in the shadows beyond, and recognise the room instantly. It's the banquet hall. And there's Armand, his sabres a blur of steel, taking on over a dozen witches. He's trying to carve his way through them to get to the Blood Countess, whose malicious laughter resonates over the sounds of combat, mocking the Hexenjäger. Behind him, Klaus and Bethlen are guarding Lieutenant Blodklutt, cutting down anything that comes near them. Klaus is still unscathed. There's not even a bead of sweat on his forehead. Bethlen, on the other hand, is covered in cuts and blood, his clothing shredded.

And then there's Blodklutt, his head still buried in the *Malleus Maleficarum*, weaving his spell. He's chanting phrases maniacally, his face drained of all its colour. Whatever he's saying, it's starting to work. Strands of blue mist

– like tentacles – are extending from the book, reaching into the furthest recesses of the room, twisting around the crones. I'm not sure what these ropes of mist will do, but the witches are terrified of them, screaming and fleeing in terror whenever they come near them.

My resolve bolstered by the fact that my companions are only yards away, I grab the witch by the neck. My fingers bite deep into her skin in an attempt to squeeze the life from her. But she wrestles free and comes at me with a fury that almost knocks me out the window, her fingernails slashing through my clothing and skin like butcher's knives. Feeling myself slip, I give a desperate cry for help. Through the witch's slashing claws, I see Armand snap around.

'Jakob! Hold on. I'm coming,' he cries, and tears forward, hacking his way through the crones, trying desperately to reach me.

He's not going to make it in time; I can no longer hold out against the witch. And so, in a last-ditch effort to prevent myself from falling, I reach out and grab her by the hair. She gives a horrific scream and tries to brace herself. But she cannot support my weight, and with a terrified cry caught in my throat, we both topple out the window.

CHAPTER TWENTY-TWO

No sooner have I slid out the window than an iron-like grip grabs me by the collar. I'm left dangling in mid-air, watching the hag – whom I release – plummet to her death. I can't drag my eyes away from her as she falls screaming down the side of the keep, her arms flailing wildly. Until there's a sickening crunch. Then silence.

I finally look away from the mangled heap, a sickness welling in my stomach. That was meant to be me. But I'm not yet out of harm's reach. On the contrary, harm has got me well and truly within its grasp. I don't even have to twist around to know that I've been caught by von Frankenthal.

He's climbed down the wall, reached out and caught me just in time.

I turn my head around to look at his face – and wish instantly that he had let me join the witch. Von Frankenthal's eyes glisten with the sadistic glee of an executioner who's been given free rein in a torture chamber. His powerful grip is like a hangman's noose and my breath comes out in constricted gasps.

I manage to wriggle my legs over to the window ledge and find purchase, releasing the pressure around my neck. I take in a few hasty gulps of air, muster what's left of my strength, and attempt to wrestle free.

Von Frankenthal watches me with morbid fascination, his iron-like grip impossible to break free of. Accepting the hopelessness of my situation, I stare in desperation through the window, searching for Armand – my last hope. But he's still a good six yards away from me, and I don't think he'll get any closer. Witches are all over him like lice on a beggar.

Then I see the Blood Countess, her back towards me, issuing commands to her coven. Her high-pitched cackle resonates through the hall as she enjoys the hold her witches have over our men. She's so caught up in her reverie that she's unaware of my presence.

I have an uninterrupted line of sight to her. It would make for a perfect shot. I would be able to kill her and break the spell she cast upon von Frankenthal, but I still haven't had a chance to reload my pistols. And with von Frankenthal grabbing my neck, I can't even reach down to draw the remaining dagger from my boot. All I have is my rapier and ... my *carbine!* I had completely forgotten about it! It is slung over my shoulder, primed and readied, left in reserve for a critical moment such as this.

With adrenalin pumping through my veins, I struggle to reach for the weapon behind my back. It takes a few tries, but once I have it I draw forth the firearm and take aim at the Countess. Seeing me retrieve my weapon, von Frankenthal squeezes harder, beads of sweat forming at his forehead. I can feel my windpipe contract, and my vision starts to blur. It will take a miracle to get this right. I pray to God I don't miss.

BLAM!

There's a powdered flash and the carbine recoils, slamming back into my shoulder, forcing me to cry out and drop the firearm. Just as the smoke starts to clear, I see the impossible happen: the Countess spins on her heel, stares at me through death-glazed eyes, then drops to the floor, black blood oozing from the hole in her head.

CHAPTER TWENTY-THREE

The instant the Countess slumps to the ground the grip around my neck relaxes, and I turn around and look up at von Frankenthal, his features as hard as granite. Thankfully, the hazy blankness is gone from his eyes, the telltale sign that he had been under the Countess's spell.

His grip weakening on the rope, he drops me through the window and climbs in after me. He then plants his massive hands on my shoulders, and lowers his head to be level with mine.

'I am in your debt, young Jakob,' von Frankenthal says, his usually stern voice soft with gratitude. 'The Blood Countess made me her puppet, and I feared I was going to slay you. I dread to think what other acts of evil she would have made me perform. But you slew the witch, and, in doing so, broke her spell and saved my life.'

I smile hesitantly in return, finding it hard to look into his eyes. 'I thought you were going to kill me,' I say, and wipe a trembling hand across my brow.

'I'm sorry,' von Frankenthal continues. 'I had no control over my actions. To be possessed by black magic and to be made a pawn of evil is to face a fate worse than death itself. All I could hope was that you would keep running, and that one of our companions would be able to slay the witch. But it was *you* who slew the Countess. For that, my young friend, I am eternally grateful. You have more than proven your worth. And if, by my life or death, I can repay you, than I shall. That is my solemn pledge.'

I don't think I've ever been more thankful in my life. Having von Frankenthal hunt me was worse than facing all of Hell's minions. It seems I have finally taken my first step in forging a friendship with the witch hunter. Armand had been correct in his assessment that the way to earn von Frankenthal's respect was to display courage. I just never thought that my first step would have to be taken under such extreme circumstances.

With the Blood Countess dead, and von Frankenthal free from her spell, we should be able to survive this nightmare. But then movement catches my eye, and I look beyond von Frankenthal. The thought of surviving Schloss Kriegsberg suddenly vanishes, and I begin to fear that the cold stone walls of the keep will serve as my tomb.

'Look out!' I say, feeling the nerves tighten in my stomach. 'We aren't out of this just yet.'

Von Frankenthal snaps his head around to see that every witch that is not actively engaged in combat with the remaining members of our company – and there are over a *dozen* of them – have fixed their eyes on me!

'I fear they wish to avenge the death of their mistress,' von Frankenthal says, arming himself with the leg of a broken chair. He shifts me away from the window and positions himself protectively in front of me. 'But all they'll find here is death. Stay behind me, young Jakob. Let me repay the debt I owe you.'

'There are too many of them!' I breathe and, drawing my rapier and dagger, prepare myself for what I'm sure will be our last stand.

This entire day has been one never-ending process of jumping out of frying pans into fires. But this time I fear I may have jumped straight into Hell's inferno. Surrounded, and pinned against the wall, there's no hope of flight. And I'm so tired I can barely muster the strength to raise my blade, let alone take on over a dozen crones.

We manage to shuffle further away from the window, and I brace my back against the wall. Then the witches tear into us like a thousand carving knives.

Von Frankenthal gives a mighty roar and lunges forward, intercepting the brunt of the witches' assault. Swinging wildly with his yard of wood, his lips turned back in a fit of rage, he shatters the jaw of one hag. No sooner has that witch toppled screaming to the floor than another leaps forward. Von Frankenthal lashes out again, a vicious punch turning the hag's face into a bloodied mess. Then more witches tear into him, their rage seemingly stoked by the fires of Hell, and it's only a matter of time before von Frankenthal is knocked back by the fury of their assault. Losing his footing, he's slammed back against the wall.

Without a moment's hesitation I dive into the fray, placing myself between von Frankenthal and the crones. It's almost as if I'm being driven by some spirit that has taken control of my body, forcing me to put aside my fear, and to pay scant regard for my own safety. I slash wildly at the first hag to emerge from the screaming mass, leaving her writhing on the floor, clutching at the gaping wound in her neck. I follow up that attack with a dagger thrust into the chest of the next hag to come forward. As she drops screaming to the ground, I lunge with my rapier at another crone's head. But she weaves past my blade, gets through my guard, and launches at my face.

Giving an involuntary cry of alarm, I stagger back and try to ward the crone away. But she's come so close that my rapier is ineffective. And so – just as she grabs me by the shoulders and opens her maw in preparation to rip into my neck – I thrust upwards with my dagger, driving it deep under her chin.

Blood, thick and warm, spills all over my hand. But the witch doesn't drop dead. To my horror, she pushes me over to the window, forces back my head, exposing the soft flesh of my neck, and has a second attempt at trying to tear into me.

'Von Frankenthal!' I cry out in anguish, hoping he can come to my rescue.

Trying desperately to keep the witch at bay, I manage to see von Frankenthal in the corner of my eye. At that instant, a terrible awareness of my impending death dashes any hope of surviving this encounter. For von Frankenthal has been dragged to the floor, smothered in witches, like ravens squabbling over carrion. There are so many, in fact, that I can barely see him.

Somewhere off to my right I can hear Armand, battling his way through the crones, calling out my name. But I fear that even he won't make it to me in time, as he too is facing some half a dozen witches. There's no sign of Klaus or Bethlen coming to save me either.

Once again, I'm left to fend for myself. And so I do all that I really can in this situation: I drive my dagger deeper into the crone's chin and try to push her away. Repulsed, I try to twist my head away, but she's too strong. At the very moment that her slavering mouth reaches my neck, and she bares her rotten teeth in preparation to sink into my flesh, a rifle report cracks over the sounds of combat.

WHAT!?

The witch snaps back violently, a cloud of pink mist bursting from the rear of her head. Blood gushes from the gunshot wound in her forehead and her crazed eyes roll back.

I push her aside and spare a stunned glance over my shoulder, out the window – to the gunpowder smoke trailing from the window in the tower rising from the opposite battlement. The tower to which *Robert Monro* had been assigned.

The Scot! Assigned to sniper duty by Captain Faust. Ordered to watch over us with his high-powered rifle. I had completely forgotten about him.

Why didn't he come to my rescue before? Didn't he see me being attacked by the other witch earlier? Though, I shouldn't complain. He did save my life just now and that's something to be grateful for.

I wave over to Robert to show my gratitude, and notice that he seems to be distracted by something. He keeps looking over his shoulder, scanning the southern slope of Brocken Mountain, almost as if he's monitoring someone's approach.

But then a commanding voice orders the witches to withdraw, bringing my attention back to the room, where a shadowy figure has entered from the adjoining stairwell.

The witches fall back from the fray, their evil cackles muted as they gaze in fear at the stranger striding into the room – a man clad in the garb of a *witch hunter*. Like no other I've seen before.

⚔ CHAPTER ⚔
TWENTY-FOUR

Thank God!

I have no idea as to who this man is, but I feel like running over and kissing his feet. He could not have arrived at a more crucial time.

Although it's obvious that this man is a witch hunter, his clothing reveals that he is not part of our order. He is decked out in the full panoply of God's holy arsenal. A rapier jostles by his side, and a pair of long-barrelled duelling pistols are tucked into his belt. What appears to be a copy of the *Malleus Maleficarum* hangs in a leather case slung over his shoulder. Crucifixes are tattooed on every part of his exposed flesh. His features are hidden in shadow beneath a wide-brimmed hat, and he is framed by a cloak as black as sin. He looks like the ultimate warrior of Christ, guaranteed to send witches running for their lives with one mere glance.

I stagger away from the window, help von Frankenthal to his feet, and then move over to join Armand. 'The reinforcements have arrived,' I say, elated. 'We've made it.'

'I wouldn't be celebrating just yet,' Armand whispers, eyeing the stranger warily. 'This smells of witchery.'

'What?'

'Something's not right here. Look at his eyes.'

I pry deep into the shadows beneath the witch hunter's hat, but I can't see anything out of the ordinary. Perhaps the fatigue of battle has started to cloud Armand's judgement and made him start to see things. I'm about to tell Armand that he must be mistaken, but then the witch hunter cranes his head around the hall, allowing light to spill under his hat, and I finally catch a glimpse of his eyes. At that very moment, my heart misses a beat, for his eyes are white!

It's only now I also notice that the witches haven't fallen back in fear of the stranger, but stepped back in reverence.

My hope sinks like an anchor. What new peril is this? The Devil masquerading as a witch hunter?

The stranger moves into the centre of the hall, and stops beside the body of the Countess. He kneels down, caresses her forehead, then embraces her still form. An eternity seems to pass before he rises again. He looks around the room, his eyes blazing with rage, hunting for the one responsible.

'Who did this?' he demands, his voice as ominous as the gates of Hell being cracked open.

In response, the witches turn and point at *me*. Right now would be a good moment for the earth to open up and swallow me whole. But there's nowhere left to run. And when the witch hunter sets his deathly stare upon me, it takes every ounce of my willpower not to fall trembling to my knees.

'I will make you feel such pain you will curse the day you were born!' the witch hunter snarls. 'I curse you and your family. You shall pay for this.'

Armand steps forward, placing himself between me and the stranger. He casts an uneasy glance over at Blodklutt, as if assessing how long he'll have to stall events before the Lieutenant's incantation is complete. And by the looks of it, it won't be long now. Blodklutt is in a trance-like state, chanting verses from the *Malleus Maleficarum*, deep within his spell. Brought to life by the magic of the Hammer of the Witches, the blue tentacles of mist are weaving around the room, and starting to lash out at the witches like striking snakes. Keeping their distance, the witches retreat to the furthest corners of the room, from where they scream at us with unbridled hatred.

'You'll need to get past me first,' Armand says, turning his attention back to the stranger. 'So the Countess took you as her groom, Heinrich von Dornheim.' He pauses, reading the flash of surprise in the former witch hunter's eyes. 'Don't look so surprised that I know your identity. Who else has their entire body tattooed with crucifixes? It must be some sort of family obsession; your father – the late Witch Bishop of Bamberg – couldn't help but adorn his witches' torture chamber with biblical texts. And so, naturally, you took it one step further.'

My eyes flash with recognition as I recall what Klaus had told me about the company of witch hunters that had entered these mountains last year. They had been sent by the Church to hunt and slay a coven of witches that had taken residence in an abandoned castle. And they had been led by Heinrich von Dornheim, the son of Johann Georg Fuchs von Dornheim, the Witch Bishop of Bamberg – one of the most infamous witch hunters to have ever lived. Heading a special witch-hunting bureaucracy, the Witch Commission, Fuchs von Dornheim had conducted a reign of terror throughout the Franconian Bishopric of Bamberg. In a five-year period, between 1626 and 1630, over six hundred people had been persecuted, tortured in Fuchs von Dornheim's special witch-prison, the Drudenhaus, and sentenced to death by being burned alive. But Fuchs von Dornheim had made the fatal error of targeting people in positions of power, and they, in turn, complained to the Pope and the Holy Roman Emperor. Held accountable for his actions, Fuchs von Dornheim fled Bamberg, and died in exile some years later. And so ended the reign of one of Franconia's most fanatical and brutal witch hunters.

'At first I was surprised to see you – alive, that is,' Armand continues. 'But now it's all starting to make sense. The famous witch hunter, Heinrich von Dornheim, is sent into the Harz Mountains to kill Countess Gretchen Kraus. Instead he is so enchanted by her beauty that he promises her not only his heart but also his immortal soul, forsaking all that is sacred, to enter an unholy union with one of the Devil's concubines. But you need not fear about losing your beloved Countess, for you will shortly join her. That, I promise you.'

No sooner has Armand finished his threat, however, than the hall erupts in chaos. Von Dornheim raises a hand and mutters something. It sounds as if he's speaking in tongues. The next instant, rippling veins of black lightning shoot forth from his fingertips. They smash into Armand and lift him off his feet, throwing him back onto me.

At the very same instant that Armand and I hit the floor, Lieutenant Blodklutt completes his incantation. The blue tentacles of mist extending from the *Malleus Maleficarum* lash out at the witches with incredible speed, latch around them, then drag them, kicking and screaming, to the centre of the hall, where the *Malleus Maleficarum* awaits. The tentacles retract into the book, dragging the hags down to their doom. It only takes a few seconds, then it's all over.

I'm left gaping, it all happened so fast. Blodklutt, having finished his incantation, collapses on the floor, clearly exhausted from the gruelling ordeal.

I stagger to my feet and look around the silent hall, feeling like the survivor of some cataclysmic event. All the witches have been dragged into the *Malleus Maleficarum*, and there's no sign of von Dornheim. In all of the screaming and confusion I lost sight of him. I can only assume that he, too, was caught by the Lieutenant's spell and destroyed.

Von Frankenthal is a few yards off to my left, his clothing shredded and stained in blood. His hands are planted on his knees, and he's sucking in air. Klaus, who is unscathed, is standing with Bethlen near Blodklutt, where they had maintained a ring of steel around him throughout the entire fight. And then there's Armand, lying on the ground near my feet. He's as charred as a singed log, his hair standing on end, wafts of smoke rising from his clothes. As torn and battered as he is, it hasn't dampened his spirit.

'Now that wasn't too difficult, was it?' he says, looking up at me, trying to maintain a brave facade, but flinching in pain against his wounds. 'Just an average day when you join the Hexenjäger.'

I offer a helping hand and pull him to his feet. 'I can't believe we're still alive,' I say, shaking my head.

With the witches, the Blood Countess and von Dornheim finally killed, and the rush of combat subsiding, I'm surprised to find that I'm not assailed by the same sensation of nausea I had experienced back in the courtyard. Perhaps the spirit of a great witch hunter lies within me after all.

But I know it's going to take a long time before I become accustomed to combat and the sight of death for, try as I may, I cannot stop my hands from trembling. Embarrassed by the involuntary shaking, I sheathe my rapier and conceal my hands within the folds of my cloak.

'We're only alive because of your efforts,' von Frankenthal says, coming over and giving me an encouraging pat on the back. 'Had you not slain the Countess, I fear we would have perished in this hall. You have the courage of a man twice your age, young Jakob. We're just lucky that you were selected to come on this mission.'

'Christian is correct,' Armand adds, sheathing his sabres. 'We owe our lives to you. For an initiate, untrained in the art of fighting witches and dark magic, you have performed deeds today that will be talked about for years to come. As I told you before, I believe you have found your calling.'

I smile warmly in return and discover, much to my surprise, that their words of encouragement have steadied my hands. My efforts today have not gone unrewarded, and I have now forged two friendships within the Hexenjäger. I think it will be a long time before I hear any favourable words from Bethlen. He's pulled up a seat on the opposite side of the central table, and is tending to a deep gash on his right thigh. I can see that he is watching me through the corner of his eye, a brooding scowl upon his face, obviously resentful of the praise I have received. Again, I find myself regretting the lies I told in order to be admitted into the Hexenjäger. If I could tell him the truth about my past, I'm sure it would bridge the gap between us; let him know that, had I not had the fortune of being adopted by a caring uncle, I would have become a street urchin. But Bethlen's resentment towards me is so great that, rather than drawing us closer, he would use this information to get me expelled from the order. Of that, I have no doubt. And so I must keep the truth of my letter of introduction carefully guarded, and try to find some other means of bridging the gap between us. I just don't know what else I can do. He's even resentful of the fact that I saved his life.

The throbbing pain in my shoulder draws me from my thoughts. Blood has seeped through the bandage, and I'm tearing a fresh replacement from my shredded tabard when my attention is drawn to Klaus. He's moved over to stand near the hearth, and is keeping a careful eye on us as he reloads his pistol. A cold shudder runs the length of my spine, as I only now remember that he is our enemy, forced into an alliance of convenience in order to defeat the Countess. Now that the Countess and her coven have been eliminated, it will only be a matter of time before we return to where we left off. And by the way in which Klaus is readying his weapons, he intends to catch us off-guard.

I shoot an anxious look at my companions, but they seem to have completely forgotten about the threat posed by Klaus. Rather than reloading their pistols and preparing for further combat, they are recovering from the fight with the coven, tending to their wounds and trying to regain their strength.

I'm about to call out to them, to draw their attention to Klaus, when I hear an ominous voice coming from the shadowed doorway of the stairwell. As one, we turn and stare at the figure emerging from the darkness. No – it cannot be! Heinrich von Dornheim's piercing white eyes are ablaze with a newfound fury.

CHAPTER TWENTY-FIVE

oncealed within the folds of his cloak, von Dornheim is reading from the leather-bound volume previously slung over his shoulder – a volume, which I only now realise is not a copy of the *Malleus Maleficarum*, but a grimoire.

Although I don't know much about dark magic, I overheard a conversation between two Hexenjäger in the communal eating hall during my first night at Burg Grimmheim. Their topic of conversation had been grimoires – Satan's unholy texts. From what I had heard, grimoires are evil tomes used by only the most powerful of witches and warlocks. They contain spells and instructions – usually scrawled in *blood* – for invoking demons. The most powerful known to exist are the *Clavis Salomonis* and the *Pseudomonarchia Daemonum*.

I'm not sure which grimoire von Dornheim is holding, but it must be powerful in order to have protected him from the *Malleus Maleficarum*. By the way he's reading from its pages, he intends to cast some diabolical spell upon us.

Our injuries and exhaustion suddenly forgotten, we gather in the centre of the hall. There's a hiss of steel as blades, still slick with blood, are drawn. Blodklutt clambers to his feet, his features strained with exhaustion. But his eyes are alert, attuned to the severity of our situation, and he readies his rapier and calls for us to gather near him.

'Well, we're not out of this yet,' Armand says, moving to the front of our party, his drawn sabres being the first line of defence against von Dornheim.

'Aye, it seems we have to face yet another foe,' Blodklutt says, and returns the *Malleus Maleficarum* to the protective leather case hanging from his belt. 'This time we won't be able to rely upon the *Malleus Maleficarum* to protect us. I'm exhausted. It will be some time before I can summon the strength to use its magic again. We'll have to rely upon our blades to fight our way out of this situation.'

'Then so be it,' von Frankenthal snarls, his brooding eyes locked on von Dornheim. 'Let's rush the witch hunter – slay him before he completes his spell. What say you, Armand and –'

He lets his sentence hang unfinished when he looks across at Klaus, only now remembering that he is in fact the Holy Spirit, our sworn enemy.

In return, Klaus curses and slashes his rapier through the air in frustration. 'So we are forced to join forces again,' he says, spitting the words with distaste.

'We'll deal with the witch hunter first,' Blodklutt says. 'Agreed? Then you and I will settle our own score.'

Klaus stares at the Lieutenant with eyes that could kill. Anxious seconds pass before he finally nods and smiles, as if savouring taking the Lieutenant's life.

'We have a deal, Papist,' he snarls. 'I will take your life first. Then I'll deal with the others.'

'So be it,' Blodklutt says, drawing his remaining pistol, and cocking back the firing pin. 'But Christian is correct. We have to get that book from von Dornheim. Either that, or kill him. He'll summon one of Hell's lieutenants if we're not careful.'

'And if that happens, we might as well start getting our coffins sized,' Armand adds grimly.

Unsettled by the fact that someone as skilled with a blade as Armand has doubts, I say a hasty prayer and cross myself. I then set my eyes upon von Dornheim, wipe the perspiration from my palms, and readjust the grip on my rapier.

Just as we're about to rush von Dornheim, he finishes reading from the grimoire, looks up and smiles evilly.

✝

I snap my head around the hall, half expecting a demon to emerge from a shadowed corner. And, as if on cue, I see it.

A *demon!*

It appears out of nowhere, over by the hearth. It is disoriented, thank God, struggling to comprehend its surroundings, obviously suffering from some form of summoning sickness.

The only demons I have seen up until this moment have been in books with pictures depicting Hell. They have been archetypal demons, with horns and pitchforks, which they have used to prod sinners as they are herded across brimstone landscapes. But nothing could prepare me for an encounter with a real demon.

It's naked, and stands over six feet tall. It has cloven feet, is rippling with muscle, and flames lick across its charcoal-coloured skin. A repugnant smell – a cross between a charnel house and sulphur – accompanies its presence, and its forked tail, over a dozen yards long, slashes through the air like a fiery whip. Its flat, flared nostrils snort the air with a squelching sound, like a blade being wrenched from the chest of an impaled foe.

Stricken with terror, I slump to my knees. Why should we even bother trying to fight this nightmare? The witches were hard enough. We won't stand a chance against this beast.

'Not now,' Blodklutt says, reaching down and hauling me to my feet. 'Do not give in to despair. There is hope yet.

It will require all of our blades to slay the demon – even yours.'

The Lieutenant's words do little to inspire hope, for I fear the demon will massacre us. What chance do we possibly have in fighting such a monstrosity? The involuntary shaking starts in my hands. I'm overcome by such despair that my throat constricts, and I find it difficult to breathe.

'It can be killed,' Blodklutt continues. 'Our weapons can harm it on hallowed ground, and I saw an old chapel in the main courtyard. We lure it there, and we can kill it.'

A spark of hope. Yet it's so dim and feeble that the shadow of evil threatens to extinguish it even before it can develop into a flame. Though it is a spark, nonetheless, and it manages to drag me out of my despair; makes me grip my rapier with renewed determination, driven by the slim chance of survival.

But any hope of making it to the chapel in time is stopped by Heinrich von Dornheim. He's standing in the doorway, his rapier drawn in preparation for combat. His intention is obvious: to keep us penned in whilst the demon tears us to shreds.

'He's cut off our only means of escape!' I cry, and point towards the former witch hunter with my rapier.

The words have barely left my mouth before Blodklutt steps forward. Without a moment's hesitation, he takes aim with his pistol – and before von Dornheim has time to respond – fires.

Von Dornheim's head jolts back, and the hat is torn from his head. For a moment he stands there, and I worry that the Lieutenant's shot has missed its mark, only grazed the witch hunter's head. But then he takes a few tottering steps on buckling legs, his arms flailing by his sides, before he slumps to the ground, dead, blood oozing from the gaping hole in his head.

It all happens within a split second, so fast that the sneer is still on the witch hunter's lips.

'There – dealt with,' Blodklutt says nonchalantly, as if killing von Dornheim was no more of a challenge than blowing his nose. He returns the pistol to his belt and draws his rapier. 'Now's our chance – before the demon comes to its senses. *Run!*'

I will my legs to move, but they are unresponsive. I'm still struggling to come to terms with what I just witnessed. Heinrich von Dornheim – who looked as if he could single-handedly wage war against Heaven – was just killed by a single pistol shot to the head! The Lieutenant made it look so easy.

'Jakob! Move!' Blodklutt barks, and shoves me in the back, propelling me forward.

The urgency in his voice draws me back to my senses, and I take a few involuntary steps forward before the severity of our situation kicks in. And then I start to sprint from the hall as if Satan's hounds were at my heels. Armand is the first to reach the doorway, and I see him dexterously reach down in mid-flight, snatching the grimoire from von Dornheim's grasp before he dashes down the stairwell.

I follow after him, only a few steps behind, taking the steps five at a time, struggling to keep pace with only one boot. My remaining companions are only a second behind me, determined to reach the chapel before . . .

Too late!

A bloodcurdling roar reverberates down the stairwell, practically sending the shadows scurrying in fright.

The demon has come to its senses.

Only a second later, over the sounds of our scuffing shoes and clinking weapons, do I hear it: a frantic clop, clop, clop. The sound is coming from above us; from the banquet hall, to be precise. It sounds like a galloping horse. How could that be? Not unless one of the Riders of the Apocalypse has also been summoned.

But then I remember the demon's cloven feet, and realise that the beast is racing across the banquet hall's flagstone floor – coming after us.

CHAPTER TWENTY-SIX

Spurred by the sounds of pursuit, we burst out of the stairwell and race along the corridor. Reaching the end of the corridor, we barge open the keep door. Then it's straight across the courtyard, straight to the ...

The chapel! Where is it? I can't see it. Nor can Armand, judging from the way in which he has come to a sudden halt, and is twisting around indecisively. There's the stable and storerooms. And over there's the granary. But there's no sign of a chapel! Could it be that Blodklutt was mistaken – that there isn't a chapel, and that he has led us to our deaths?

But then the Lieutenant exits the keep and races off to the left. He calls after us, directing us towards a rundown building tucked under the battlements. It doesn't look much larger than a hovel, and the only visible indicator that it is a place of worship is the crucifix askew on the roof. It must have just enough room to accommodate an altar and the odd pew. Most importantly, it's hallowed ground, the only place we're going to be able to face the demon – our only hope of survival. And so we race over to it. With the exception of Klaus, we are a procession of wounded, desperate men, nursing injuries and lathered in a mixture of sweat and blood. All driven by a will to survive, forcing us to keep moving, to make it to the safety of the chapel.

Blodklutt is the first to reach the building, and he shoulders open the door and rushes inside. I follow straight after him, racing into the gloom beyond, paying a cursory glance at the room's layout. I was correct in my assumption that the chapel was small. It is some twelve yards wide, and only a little longer. Three pews, rotten and broken with age, are positioned in the centre of the room. An altar, with an alcove and statue located behind it, stands in the shadows on the far side of the room.

'The door!' Blodklutt calls out as the rest of our company assembles in the chapel. 'We must barricade it. Here – this pew. Help me move it.'

We rush over to the pew. Despite its broken-down condition, it's incredibly heavy, and it takes four of us to move it. Having braced it against the door, barricading ourselves inside, we step back and ready our weapons. Trying to regain our breath, our hearts beating wildly, we stare expectantly at the door, waiting for the demon to reach the chapel.

There's the sound of Bethlen's heavy breathing, and Armand clicking his tongue. And then comes the sound of movement from outside. By the sound of it, the demon is moving impossibly fast, racing across the courtyard, coming straight at us.

CRASH! The demon throws itself against the door. Heavy nail-studded oak beams splinter like toothpicks. The pew is knocked back. But the iron cross-pieces keep the door intact.

The door has withstood the demon's fury, kept it at bay. But it won't hold against a second charge. Realising this, and hoping that their bulk and strength will be able to bolster the door, von Frankenthal and Bethlen race over and throw their shoulders against it.

Against any other foe, I'm sure von Frankenthal's and Bethlen's massive frames would be enough. But we are facing no ordinary enemy, and I fear that even von Frankenthal's shoulders will be as ineffective in holding out the demon as trying to plug a burst dam with a pebble.

'Hold it for as long as you can,' Blodklutt says, and gestures for the rest of us to reload our firearms. 'Buy us enough time to ready our pistols. It will be best if we can take this beast out before it gets in close.'

'We'll give you as long as you need,' von Frankenthal says, and draws a dagger from his belt in preparation for close-quarters combat.

Klaus, however, flourishes his rapier and scoffs at Lieutenant Blodklutt. He then takes off his hat, tosses it aside, and pushes past von Frankenthal and Bethlen to take a position by the door.

'Steel is all I need,' he boasts, looking back at us contemptuously. 'Why don't you Papal scum just cower at the back?' He peers through a crack in the door. 'I'll take the beast. I'll meet it with drawn steel. So move away and give me room. And I swear – once I finish with the demon, then I'll deal with you. This has dragged on long enough.'

Von Frankenthal doesn't respond to the Holy Spirit's comment. He just shoots him a disgusted look, and manages to reposition himself at the side of the door. 'Get ready!' he warns shortly, looking through a crack between the door and the wall. 'The demon's going to charge again.'

I don't think anything could prepare us for what happens next. Before any of us could notice, Bethlen draws himself up behind Klaus . . . and drives his rapier into his back.

CHAPTER TWENTY-SEVEN

K laus gives a bloodcurdling cry and his body arches violently. He claws desperately at the door, writhing in pain against the blade driven into his back. But Bethlen is merciless, and he drives his blade deeper, until only the hilt remains visible. Klaus's body contorts in pain until he slumps against the door to which he has been impaled.

'Consider our alliance void,' Bethlen says, extracting his blade and sneering sadistically as Klaus drops lifeless to the floor. 'At least he's one problem we no longer have to worry about. So much for the Holy Spirit.'

We stand speechless, staring at Bethlen. Despite the fact that we knew we would eventually have to fight Klaus, none of us suspected that Bethlen would slay him in this manner. Yes, Klaus was a member of the Brotherhood of the Cross, a sworn enemy of the Roman Catholic Church. The Brotherhood was responsible for the deaths of over a hundred people. They had even targeted our order over the course of the past few months. But that did not mean that Klaus should have died with a sword driven into his back. There had been neither skill, nor courage, involved in his death. All that had been required was a cold-blooded heart.

Raised on the streets of Mannheim, Bethlen had had to fight for everything in life, even if it meant performing deeds which many would consider heartless. A window of opportunity presented itself when Klaus turned his back, and Bethlen, driven by the same instincts that allowed him to survive as a child on the crime-infested alleyways of Mannheim, had simply seized it.

The moment he drove his blade into Klaus's back, however, I realised that Bethlen and I are nothing alike. I had previously believed that, had it not been for my uncle who had rescued me from the streets and took me under his wing, I would have become like Bethlen, angry, and desperate for more than life had presented me with. I now know that's not the case. Irrespective of how desperate a situation becomes, I will never compromise the values of compassion, mercy and honour. I could have never stabbed Klaus through the back. Although he was an enemy, he should not have been robbed of an honourable death.

In his foolish actions, Bethlen also paid scant regard to the fact that we needed Klaus's blade. The Holy Spirit was a skilled swordsman, perhaps even better than Lieutenant Blodklutt and Armand, and his expertise was needed to defeat the demon. We'll need every able-bodied man on deck for the ensuing fight. I just hope that Bethlen's merciless act will not have disastrous consequences for the rest of us.

'What's done is done,' Blodklutt comments. His grim tone suggests that he, too, was unimpressed by Bethlen's brutality. 'Now ready yourselves. The demon comes!'

No sooner has the Lieutenant drawn our attention back to the demon, than – *CRASH!* The door explodes inwards and splinters of wood shower the room. We're all knocked off our feet. The blast throws von Frankenthal and me across the chapel, where we slam hard against the wall.

I slide to the floor, the wind knocked out of me. I'm vaguely aware of voices barking around me. They are desperate voices, those of men who know they are about to die. All I can see are a thousand pinpricks of silver, flashing before me like a brilliant night sky. It would be so tempting to succumb to my fatigue; to let myself fall under the bewitching spell of the stars and slip into a deep sleep. But some primal instinct forces me to regain my feet. Even in my dazed state, I am aware that I am in mortal danger.

I stagger to my feet and support myself against the wall. Trying to fight back the reeling sensation in my head, I take some deep breaths. Then, gradually, I start to come back to my senses.

I snap my head back to where the door *used* to be. It looks as if a petard went off. There's splintered wood everywhere, and a body stirs somewhere under the rubble. And then I see von Frankenthal. He's regained his feet, crossed back to the doorway, and is wrestling the demon!

Fortunately, the demon's skin is no longer rippling in flames. Perhaps it's some side effect of being on hallowed ground, stripping the demon of some of its powers. Whatever the reason, von Frankenthal isn't able to capitalise much on the situation. I've got to give him credit for trying, though. He's trying desperately to weave through the beast's defences with his dagger. But his efforts are futile. It will only be a matter of seconds until the demon tears him to shreds.

As if reading my thoughts, the demon lashes out with its tail, wraps it around von Frankenthal's legs, and – with a tremendous yank – pulls him to the ground. The demon then stands triumphantly over its helpless prey, its claws extended in preparation to dive in for the kill.

Realising that immediate action is needed, I push myself away from the wall and stumble towards the demon. I have not had any time to consider how I will draw the beast away from my stricken companion, but I know that if I do not distract it, von Frankenthal will surely die.

With no readied firearm, and knowing that I do not

have time to cross the room and engage the demon with my blade, I collect a length of wood from the floor and hurl it at the beast. Although only intended as a hasty distracting shot, the missile hits the demon square on the forehead, making it stagger back, clutching its head in pain. My effort only distracts the beast for a few seconds. Before I've had time to give any thought to how I should seize this advantage, the demon gives a demented roar, flexes its muscle-corded arms, and sets its eyes upon me.

I may have saved von Frankenthal, but I have now placed myself in extreme peril. Overcome with fear, I start to shake uncontrollably and fall to my knees. I try to call out for help, but I'm so terrified that the words get caught in my throat. I've come close to death many times today, but I fear that there will be no escape for me this time.

Out of the corner of my eye, I see Armand and Lieutenant Blodklutt emerge from the shadows behind the altar. Consumed by my need to save von Frankenthal, I had completely forgotten about my remaining companions. Whereas Bethlen lies dazed beneath the shattered remnants of the door, the Lieutenant and Armand had withdrawn to the relative safety of the far side of the chapel. There they had focused on reloading their pistols, and they brandish these as they step forward.

'Step no closer to the boy,' Blodklutt threatens, drawing the demon's attention. 'Come and face me.'

The demon stops, snaps its head to the right to consider its new opponents. Then, without even so much as a cursory glance at me, it moves towards them, confident that it will tear through them like a scythe through wheat.

It has taken no more than three steps before it hesitates. It narrows its eyes warily, evidently suspicious of the dogged witch hunters standing before it sporting triumphant grins.

For the first time, doubt registers on the demon's features, like someone who has just realised they have wandered into an assassin's trap. And only now does it see through its bloodlust and take in its surroundings, noticing that it has charged blindly into the chapel, onto *hallowed ground* – the only place where our weapons can slay it.

Lieutenant Blodklutt and Armand level their pistols and fire.

The blamming sounds of their pistols' reports are drowned by a bloodcurdling roar as the demon takes both shots square in the chest. Staggering back, it loses its footing and collapses to its knees. It clutches a hand at its chest and stares, mesmerised, at the blood – as black as oil – spilling from the gunshot wounds, flowing between its claws.

It's obvious that the demon has never before been injured. Never before has it experienced pain, seen the stain of its own blood. For the first time it has tasted the bitter poison of mortality.

It turns, looks back at the remains of the door, gauges if it has time to escape from the chapel – if it has time to flee to safety. But time is a luxury the demon doesn't have. For no sooner has the smoke cleared from their pistols than Armand and Blodklutt draw their blades and descend upon the beast in a blur of steel. At the same moment, von Frankenthal wrestles free from the beast's tail and places himself between the demon and the doorway – a final barrier of flesh and steel between the demon and its freedom.

Fighting back the wave of fear that had previously incapacitated me, I climb gingerly to my feet, force myself to aid my companions. Though it's not as if they're going to be in any need of my assistance. Before I've taken even one step, Blodklutt weaves through the demon's defences and drives his blade into its chest – deep into its heart.

The demon gives such a terrifying roar it's a miracle that the walls of the chapel don't collapse. It slides from the Lieutenant's blade to lie in a pool of its own blood.

CHAPTER TWENTY-EIGHT

With the demon slain, I sit on the floor, overcome by a mixture of exhaustion and elation. I cannot believe that the fighting has finally come to an end. I'm so relieved I feel like calling out at the top of my voice in defiance of fate.

Armand prods the demon with the toe of his boot, checking to see if it is indeed dead. Satisfied, he extracts Bethlen from beneath the door, lends him a shoulder, and assists him over to one of the pews. He then crosses over to me, slumps down by my side, and slaps me across the back.

'You've done well,' he commends. 'I'll fight by your side any day.'

I know that's a compliment, but fighting is the last thing on earth I feel like doing right now. I hope it's going to be a long time before I have to draw my sword again. I knew that when I joined the Hexenjäger I would be required to fight the forces of darkness. I just didn't expect to have to fight them *all* within the same day. I've seen enough today to make Pieter Bruegel's *The Triumph of Death* appear as a painting of a church picnic. But it's all over now. It's time to sheathe our blades, bandage our wounds, and make our way back to Burg Grimmheim for a well-earned rest.

Rest – the word seems so alien. I feel as though I've been strapped to a bolting horse all day, clinging for sheer life, hurtling along a forest path riddled with exposed roots and low-lying branches. Now the ride is finally over. And this broken-down chapel is to be where I repose. It's not exactly the sort of place I'd usually consider resting in, but beggars can't be choosers. And right now the rubble-strewn floor of the chapel is as inviting as a feather and down quilt.

I lie back down on the floor and close my eyes, suddenly aware of a million aches and pains all over my body. With the rush of combat subsiding, the wounds I have sustained are starting to register. It's funny how our bodies do that. I've heard stories of soldiers who have had an arm blown off, and yet they've managed to flee from fields of combat, only to fall dead from shock upon learning that they are missing a limb. Fortunately, I haven't been critically wounded, though I've never before felt so bruised and battered.

Movement near the doorway catches my attention. I look up to see von Frankenthal rummaging through the rubble. What's he up to? Doesn't he ever stop?

'It doesn't make any sense to waste perfectly good weapons,' he announces at length, having retrieved Klaus Grimmelshausen's blades. He tucks a dagger into his belt, then dusts off Klaus's rapier and tests its weight. 'This is a fine blade. The work of a master swordsmith. It's not very often you see a blade of this quality. The hilt appears to be of Flemish design, but the blade was fashioned in German-speaking lands – by the famous bladesmith, Tesche of Solingen, to be precise, as revealed by the surname inscribed here.' He pauses, turns and looks at me. 'You should have it.'

I shake my head and raise a hand, refusing his offer. 'A nice blade indeed, but a pawn of evil. I dread to think how many innocent lives it's stolen.'

'All the more reason why you should become its master,' Lieutenant Blodklutt says, drenching his face in water from a leather water-skin that had been hanging from his belt. 'It's not the sword that is evil, but the one who wields it. A rapier such as this – in your hands – would become an instrument of good. Besides, you've more than proven your worth today. Consider it a spoil of war.'

Bethlen raises his eyes from the pistol he's been reloading, and glares at me. Is that jealousy burning in his eyes? I wouldn't want to deny Bethlen a reward that he believes he rightfully deserves, especially if it gives him more reason to hate me. Then again, I dread to think of how many more merciless acts the blade will be put to if it ends up in his hands. I've already seen him assassinate a man from behind; it makes me wonder how many other people have suffered in Bethlen's hands.

And in that instant, I know to accept the sword. I climb to my feet and stagger over to von Frankenthal, who promptly hands me the blade and its baldric. I test the weight of the rapier, and slash it through the air for measure. I don't know too much about swords, but it feels like a fine blade indeed. I've never before seen such an elaborate hilt – comprising the wolf's-head cross-guard, a large ovoid pommel, a grip of silver twistwire and a pierced shell guard.

Not wanting to sport my new trophy in front of Bethlen, however, I sling the baldric over my shoulder, sheathe the blade, and sit down beside Armand.

'There's one thing I don't understand,' I say, drawing the Frenchman's attention. 'When we were back in the banquet hall, facing Heinrich von Dornheim, Lieutenant Blodklutt had said that he had been so drained by the *Malleus Maleficarum* that he would not be able to use it again for some time. But why couldn't someone else simply use the tome? Why must the Lieutenant bear the sole burden of using the Hammer of the Witches?'

'It takes years of training to be able to wield the magic of the *Malleus Maleficarum*,' Armand explains. 'The text was created by the German witch hunters Kramer and Sprenger as an instructive text for the detection and interrogation of witches. But they hid a secret code within their book, carefully concealed within cryptic verses. Those who know how to decipher the code are granted access to magic that can combat Satan's most powerful minions. The magic is difficult to wield – even Kramer and Sprenger were wary of unleashing its true powers. It is normal practice for at least one member of each company of Hexenjäger sent into the field to be trained in its use. In this instance, that person is Blodklutt. He is the only one here who knows how to read the cryptic verses.'

Talking about magical tomes, I cannot help but notice that the grimoire Armand collected from von Dornheim is tucked under his belt. You can practically feel the evil emanating from it. I wouldn't go near the thing even if the Pope were holding my hand. Just looking at it is enough to make me want to have a bath in holy water.

'What do you intend to do with that?' I ask, and gesture at the heavy volume.

'What any good Christian soul would do – destroy it.'

My eyes narrow inquisitively. 'And how do you destroy a grimoire?'

'Like this.'

And with that, Armand produces the evil volume. He holds it for a moment, as if savouring a sweet victory, like a general staring at the flames rising from a conquered city. Then he lets it slip from his fingers.

It hits the ground . . . and turns to *ash*.

Armand reads the astonished look on my face. 'You have a lot to learn, my young friend,' he says, and smiles softly. 'Nothing evil can withstand hallowed ground. Not even Satan could walk in here without fear of being slain.'

'Don't even joke about that,' I return. 'Given what's happened today, it wouldn't surprise me in the least if the Devil were to walk in here right now.'

As if on cue, a figure bursts through the shattered doorway.

◆CHAPTER◆
TWENTY-NINE

Despite our exhausted state, our hands fly to our weapons and we spring to our feet – only to find that Robert Monro has burst into the chapel.

'I wouldn't advise you do that again,' Armand warns, breathing a sigh of relief and re-sheathing his half-drawn sabres. 'I was about to have your head off!'

'I'm sorry, but we've got a problem,' the Scot blurts out, desperate urgency in his voice. 'A dozen horsemen are coming this way! They are armed to the teeth, and clad in blue tabards bearing fleur-de-lis.'

Lieutenant Blodklutt's head snaps up. 'Blue tabards with fleur-de-lis! I'd say we've got more than just a problem.'

Armand moans, obviously annoyed by the prospect of further fighting. 'How long do we have?'

'I've been watching their approach for some time now,'

Robert answers. 'But it's only been in the last minute that I've been able to identify their tabards. We have five minutes at the most.'

'Then that's all we need to make our escape,' Blodklutt says. 'We're in no condition to face the Marquis de Beynac. We need to move – fast!'

The mere mention of that name makes my skin crawl. I don't know much about affairs in France, but I very much doubt that there's a single person born in the past decade who has not heard of the Marquis de Beynac – Louis XIV's Master of Spies. The leader of the King's Secret – a spy network that has infiltrated every court in Europe. Nothing is kept secret from him. If knowledge is power, then he is truly the most powerful man alive.

Many counts, dukes, princes and even monarchs – fearful of state secrets falling into the wrong hands – have tried to have the Marquis de Beynac killed; they've hired some of the most skilled assassins in Europe to drive a blade into his back in the dead of night. But all attempts have failed.

Why? The answer is simple: because of the Marquis de Beynac's bodyguard, Horst von Skullschnegger. A living legend who shadows the Master of Spies' every move, it is said that von Skullschnegger has a military record that would shame even Alexander the Great. Having hired out his sword as a professional mercenary, he has fought in numerous European campaigns. Along with von Pappenheim, he was one of the greatest Catholic League cavalry captains of the Thirty Years' War. He single-handedly conquered a gun battery at White Mountain, and is rumoured to have slain Gustavus Adolphus, the Lion of the North, at the Battle of Lutzen in 1632. A close friend and personal guard of Prince Rupert, he fought in every major engagement during the English Civil War. Six horses, it is said, were shot from under him at Marston Moor. He has even served in the frontier wars against Indian tribes in America, and has written a treatise on the art of cavalry charges.

In short, think of any battle waged in the past three decades and it's a sure bet Horst von Skullschnegger was there. And I'll be the Elector of Saxony's lapdog if he isn't riding into Schloss Kriegsberg this very moment.

'I wonder what brings them here?' von Frankenthal says, assuming position in the doorway, keeping watch across the inner courtyard.

'It's no secret that Louis XIV wishes to extend the Bourbon Empire into the east,' Armand explains. 'France gained much territory from the Treaty of Westphalia, but Louis craves more. This will no doubt involve invading the western states of the Holy Roman Empire – Lorraine, Franche Comté and the Spanish Netherlands. It will be a bitter struggle. Lots of blood will be spilt. But with a weapon such as one of the Trumpets of Jericho, Louis XIV will be able to conquer all of Europe. I'm sure that's why he's here. He's come for the trumpet.'

I shake my head, struggling to understand why the Marquis de Beynac is coming to Schloss Kriegsberg. 'But the trumpet *isn't* here. It was just a ruse to draw out the Brotherhood of the Cross.'

Armand taps his nose. 'But the Marquis doesn't know that.'

'I know, and that's my point exactly,' I say, raising a hand, trying to stop Armand from following his line of thought. 'We need to take a step back here. For we are forgetting one simple question – why does the Marquis believe that this castle is the resting place of the trumpet? Someone has obviously told him that the trumpet is here. And that couldn't happen unless –'

'We'll worry about that later,' Lieutenant Blodklutt interrupts. 'Let's just focus on getting out of here for the moment.'

But I don't think any of us will be going anywhere. Not with Bethlen brandishing his pistol at us.

'Stay your hands from your weapons,' Bethlen orders. 'The first to draw their blade dies!'

'What do you think you're doing?' von Frankenthal blurts out, and takes a menacing step forward.

'Holding you here until my men arrive,' Bethlen returns, and halts von Frankenthal with the barrel of his pistol.

Huh? As far as I knew we weren't receiving any reinforcements. Then everything begins to fall into place. He is a spy. Bethlen had already known that there were others inside Schloss Kriegsberg – I saw his feigned surprise. He must have thought that the Marquis de Beynac and the King's Secret had entered the castle first. What a shock he must have got when we encountered the Brotherhood instead! The twists in this mission don't seem to end.

'Don't you think this has become a little too clichéd?' Armand says, inching closer towards Bethlen. 'Full credit goes to Klaus for bailing us up in the keep, but this is just cheap imitation.'

'Put the pistol down before I snap that lousy neck of yours!'

I cringe at von Frankenthal's words. He doesn't have a civil tongue at the best of times, and I don't think he'll be the one to defuse this situation.

Bethlen snaps the pistol between von Frankenthal and Armand. 'Be quiet! And nobody move.'

'Or what?' Blodklutt asks, composed. 'You're going to kill us all with your *sole* pistol? You must be a good shot.'

Bethlen's eyes narrow into slits devoid of compassion, and he levels his pistol at me. 'Then let me simplify matters somewhat. If anybody moves, I'll kill the whelp.'

✦CHAPTER✦
THIRTY

I t's amazing how things can go from good to bad in a split second. There I was, only a few minutes ago, celebrating – what I believed to be – the defeat of our final foe. And now I'm right back in the thick of things, staring down the barrel of Bethlen's pistol.

Armand raises a hand, cautions Bethlen not to do anything rash. 'So where do we go from here?'

'Nowhere. We simply wait,' Bethlen says, his eyes locked on mine, then shifting to the hand Armand moves to the hilt of his blade.

But I know that my companions won't allow themselves to be held up in here until the Marquis de Beynac and Horst von Skullschnegger arrive. It is in our best interests to try to escape whilst we face only one opponent.

'So how much did the Marquis offer you?' Armand asks.

'It must have been a lot to betray your companions.'

'Companions?' Bethlen snorts. 'Don't be so presumptuous.'

'It wouldn't take much to win over this dog,' von Frankenthal scoffs. 'He's probably been won over by a single coin.'

'I wasn't *won over*, you ignorant fool,' Bethlen sneers. 'I've been in the Marquis's service for over a decade.'

Von Frankenthal snorts contemptuously. 'Then that just goes to show how desperate the Marquis de Beynac must be if he has stooped to hiring dogs as his spies. He's really scraping at the bottom of the barrel.'

Bethlen's eyes flash with anger, and he redirects his pistol at von Frankenthal. 'Don't tempt me. You humiliated me yesterday. It won't happen a second time. And I don't think you're in any position to talk to me about hiring dogs. You couldn't even protect young Gerhard. He died because of your incompetence. And now,' he pauses as he snaps the pistol back at me, 'you're going to cause the death of this whelp.'

Although I'm standing several yards away from von Frankenthal, I hear his breathing become heavy and his features darken. Bethlen's words have cut deep, and von Frankenthal is trying desperately to keep his rage in check. I'm sure that the only reason why he hasn't charged Bethlen is because of the pistol trained at me.

'Besides, you know nothing of the Marquis de Beynac,' Bethlen continues. 'His arms reach into every court in

Europe, and I am one of his most experienced spies. It's no secret that your order has prioritised the recovery of ancient relics. I was sent to infiltrate the Hexenjäger on the off-chance that you would discover something that France could use to its advantage.'

'But this was all a trap – designed to draw out the Brotherhood of the Cross,' Lieutenant Blodklutt says. 'And you have also fallen for it. You must feel an absolute fool.'

Bethlen shrugs. 'It's of no consequence. For you will shortly be dead. Then I will simply return to the Hexenjäger and await another opportunity.'

Armand shakes his head in disgust. 'Are we supposed to be impressed?'

'I couldn't care less what you think, fop! And it's best if you keep your mouth closed. You've shamed the royal court of France with your libertine ways. You've also angered King Louis with your vendetta against his Musketeers. I'd be doing the King a service in killing you.'

I shake my head in disbelief and look at Bethlen imploringly. 'Why can't you just let us go? Surely your heart can't be so cold that you don't feel anything for us.'

Bethlen glares at me, and his finger tightens on the pistol trigger. 'You'd be wrong there, whelp.'

Von Frankenthal steps forward. 'I've had more of this than I can stomach,' he growls. 'We'll have no chance of flight once the Marquis arrives. It's now or never. So let's take him now – right now!'

If von Frankenthal's aim was to make Bethlen panic, then he achieved his objective. Flustered, Bethlen's eyes flash in alarm, and he aims his pistol directly at von Frankenthal. Then, for only a split second, he lets his focus stray. He makes the fatal error of glancing back at the doorway, almost as if gauging whether he has a clear line of flight from the chapel.

As soon as the pistol's aim shifts away from me, von Frankenthal reacts. His hand shoots to the dagger tucked into his belt. He pulls it out, and with a speed that defies his massive frame, he dives to the right and throws the dagger. Panicked, Bethlen cries out in alarm and shoots. But whereas Bethlen's shot misses – the ball whizzing through the air a hand's-breadth off to von Frankenthal's left – von Frankenthal's dagger sinks deep into Bethlen's chest.

At the same moment that von Frankenthal reached for his dagger, Armand and Blodklutt drew their blades. In less than a heartbeat, they streak forward and drive their swords into Bethlen's torso.

It all happens in perfect unison. So fast, in fact, that by the time I realise what has happened, Bethlen is lying in a crumpled heap on the chapel floor, staring up at the ceiling through lifeless eyes.

I stare, speechless, at Bethlen's limp form. His deception and subsequent death have left a bitter taste in my mouth.

Strangely, I don't feel any anger towards Bethlen. I would have expected that, as he had threatened to kill me, I would feel some resentment towards him. But I don't. All I feel for him is pity. Bethlen was dissatisfied with his life from the start. All he wanted was to prove to the world his worth, to rise from his impoverished childhood and accomplish much more than what was socially expected of him. He was prepared to make any bargain and betray any trust in his pursuit of that goal. But, sadly, he went the wrong way about achieving it. He lived and died by the sword.

I remind myself that, like Bethlen, my own position in this order is based on lies, but unlike him my deception was not as extreme and vindictive. I would like to think that the friendships I have formed with Armand and von Frankenthal are based on honesty, even though I gained their trust under false pretenses. And as stronger bonds of friendship are formed, heavier grows the guilt on my conscience.

I'm drawn from my thoughts by Lieutenant Blodklutt. He reaches down, retrieves Bethlen's pistol and rapier, and hands them to von Frankenthal.

'Let's not linger,' he warns. 'That shot may have alerted the Marquis.'

An unexpected noise in the courtyard prompts von Frankenthal to rush towards the door. Immediately, he withdraws from the doorway and braces his back against the wall, his face ashen.

'It's too late,' he warns. 'They're here!'

⟻CHAPTER⟼
THIRTY-ONE

'They're fanning out across the courtyard, encircling our position,' von Frankenthal says, spying through the doorway. 'I don't think they intend for us to walk out of here.'

Armand positions himself beside von Frankenthal, and peers into the courtyard. 'The Marquis de Beynac doesn't do anything in half measures. So what's the plan?'

'We rush them. Take the fight to them. I'm not going to die in here like some caged rat.'

I don't intend to die like a rat either, von Frankenthal. But I don't see how tearing into the courtyard – to be riddled with musket fire and skewered with rapiers – is a preferable option. We'd be cut to shreds the second we set foot outside the chapel. Sometimes a few thoughtful words can defuse a volatile situation. But not so with von

Frankenthal. I imagine he's the sort of person who would more readily draw his blade than make any attempt at diplomacy. He always takes the aggressive option, and probably considers negotiations only for the faint of heart. Needless to say, I don't think there's much fight left in me. If we can somehow negotiate with the Marquis de Beynac for our safe release from this chapel, then I'm all for that. And I know just the man for the job: Armand, with his rogue's silver tongue.

'I wonder if they'll be open to negotiations,' Armand says, as if reading my thoughts. 'A few polite words may save us from unnecessary bloodshed.'

'I'll second that,' I say eagerly.

Lieutenant Blodklutt moves over to one of the chapel's windows and stares through the filthy panes into the court-yard. He then withdraws and starts to reload his pistol. 'It may be too late for that. But I suppose we don't have many other options. Armand – are you feeling up to the task?'

Armand brushes back his hair and adjusts his torn, bloodstained collar. He's so bruised and battered he'd be banned from participating in rising with the dead on Judgement Day. Nonetheless, he winks at Blodklutt, raises his chin with pride, produces his bloodstained handker-chief and gives it a dramatic flourish. 'Of course. This will be easier – dare I say – than stealing a kiss from a maiden.'

He's not lacking in confidence – I'll give him that. But I don't know how successful he's going to be. It's not as if we have much to bargain with. In fact, we have *nothing* to bargain with. We don't have the Scourge of Jericho in our possession. We can't even exchange Bethlen for our release. We're not exactly in the best position to open negotiations. It would be like trying to bluff your way through a game of cards with the lowest hand possible.

But we've got no other option, and so out steps Armand, dirtier than a street urchin, to plea for our lives.

Armand has barely emerged from the chapel – hasn't even had the opportunity to say a single word – before a voice cries out from the opposite side of the courtyard.

'*Fire!*'

This is followed instantly by a salvo of musket and pistol fire. The noise is deafening! It sounds as if there are over a hundred guns out there. The chapel's windows shatter, spraying glass through the air. Armand scurries back into the chapel, dives for safety under a pew, and screams out that even dogs have more honour than the Frenchmen who opened fire on him.

I dive instinctively to the ground, shield my eyes and scramble across the floor. There are shards of glass everywhere, and I grit my teeth in pain as I try to move deeper into the chapel. A few more yards and I'm finally free of the glass. I open my eyes, and find myself staring at someone's feet. My head snaps up in alarm, but then I give a sigh of relief, for it's only the Virgin Mary. Well, at least, a *statue* of the Virgin Mary, hidden in the shadowed alcove at the rear of the chapel, behind the altar.

My eyes are drawn to an inscription, carved in Latin, at the base of the statue – an inscription that fills me with hope. For when I travelled to Rome with Father Giuseppe Callumbro, I saw this same inscription carved into the pedestal of a similar statue, in the basilica of Saint Sebastian.

Ad catacumbas. Translation – in the hollows. Marking the entrance to Rome's catacombs.

I don't know exactly why anybody would have carved '*ad catacumbas*' into the base of this statue. The inscription in the basilica of Saint Sebastian was used as a marker to indicate the entrance to the Christian catacombs: a subterranean labyrinth in which the early Christians, defying the Roman custom of cremation, had buried their dead. But Schloss Kriegsberg is a medieval construction, built over a thousand years *after* the birth of Christ. And it certainly isn't part of the Roman catacomb network. So why, then, use the same inscription?

It's not uncommon for castles and palaces to have secret escape routes. Sliding wall panels, false bookcases – even wells – often grant access to secret passages that lead to safe-points beyond the castle. Just as the early Christians had used the catacombs to hide from the Romans during times of persecution, I'm hoping that this inscription reveals the location of an underground escape passage.

There's only one way to find out. And so I leap to my feet and spit into my hands. I then take a deep breath, muster my resolve, and throw myself – hard! – against the statue. I push with all my might, but it feels as if the statue weighs a ton. I might as well be trying to push over one of the Egyptian pyramids! It's not long before the blood is hammering in my temples. After what seems to be an eternity, I finally manage to shift the statue a few feet to the right.

I step back, try to regain my breath, and notice that the wide base of the statue had covered a narrow flight of stairs, barely three feet wide, and descending into darkness. I punch a hand into the air in victory. I was right. There is a concealed entrance, offering perhaps our only means of escape.

I call out to my companions.

'Well done, young Jakob,' Armand says, scurrying over. 'How did you ever find this?'

'I'll tell you later,' I say. 'Let's just get out of here for now.'

Lieutenant Blodklutt stares down into the darkness, his eyes shining with newfound hope. 'Jakob – you lead. Then Christian and Armand. Robert and I will take the rear.'

Without a second to lose, I make my way carefully down the stairs. I have barely moved down a few yards before it becomes so dark that I can hardly see where I'm going. This isn't good. If we don't have light we'll trip and break our necks.

But I see the torch, placed in a bracket on the wall to my left. Saying a silent prayer, I light the torch with my tinder and flint, and then snatch it from the wall. Then it's straight down the stairs, straight into the . . . cobwebs! This would be a fly's worst nightmare. And the smell is terrible. The air's so stale you don't want to breathe. You can practically taste it.

I reach the bottom of the stairs and enter a long passageway, some three yards wide, carved into the stone foundations of the castle. I race along this new passage, von Frankenthal, an avalanche of muscle, following only a step behind me. Then there's Armand, urging us forward, deeper into the darkness. Finally, Blodklutt and Robert bring up the rear, casting fearful glances over their shoulders, wary of just how long we have before the Marquis de Beynac learns of our escape. For, when he does, he'll send his troops – led by Horst von Skullschnegger – to hunt us down. And in our exhausted state, there's only one way that scenario will end.

In a *bloodbath*.

CHAPTER THIRTY-TWO

We move through the tunnel as fast as we can. Our laboured breaths and the scrape of our swords against the stone walls reverberate in the narrow passage. But these sounds are drowned by the all-too-regular curses emitted by von Frankenthal as he crashes his head against the roof. He'd better be careful or he'll leave a trail of blood for the Marquis's troops to follow. Needless to say, it's not as if they are going to need to follow a trail to work out which way we've gone. There have been no side-passages, no alternate routes; just the stairs, and then one long, straight passage through the darkness. We have been presented with no opportunities to throw the Marquis off our trail. All we can do is put as much distance between the Marquis and ourselves as possible – and find, I'm hoping, an exit from the passage. Then we'll disappear into the forested slopes of the Harz Mountains, never to be seen in this area again.

It sounds all too simple. But even the simplest of plans comes to an abrupt halt when you find your escape route blocked by a lowered *metal portcullis.*

Trapped!

And at that very moment, we hear cries of alarm echo down through the tunnel. The Marquis de Beynac has entered the chapel and learned of our escape – meaning that we may have only seconds before he discovers the secret passage.

We have to move – *fast.*

I try lifting the portcullis, only to find that it's stuck fast. But we can't get caught here. Not now. Not after all we've been through today. There has to be a way to get out of here.

I start looking for a mechanism – a release catch – that will raise the iron gate. Von Frankenthal pushes past me, flexes his massive arms, and throws himself against the barrier – two hundred and fifty pounds of corded muscle against two hundred pounds of riveted iron. The veins in his neck look as if they're about to pop out of his skin. You could practically tight-rope walk across them. But not even von Frankenthal's prodigious strength is enough to raise the portcullis. After several seconds he slumps back, exhausted, defeated.

'Can we get through?' Lieutenant Blodklutt's voice is a desperate whisper from behind.

'I'm working on it,' I say, probing my torch into the darkness on either side of the barrier, searching for a release catch. There's nothing but chiselled stone.

'Well, whatever you're going to do, you'd better do it fast,' Robert says. 'They've discovered the tunnel.'

No sooner have the words left the Scot's mouth than sounds of pursuit carry down the passage: the clink of weapons, a cough, and the muffled scrape of footsteps; telltale signs that the Marquis's troops are descending the stairs into the tunnel.

Panic starts to set in. My pulse quickens and the hairs on my arms stand erect. I still can't see any sign of a release mechanism.

'Extinguish the torch,' Blodklutt commands. 'Don't make us easier targets than we already are.'

I have one last desperate search, but can't see anything. I then stamp out the torch, and start groping along the walls in the darkness, still searching in vain for the elusive release catch.

'We're going to hold them off whilst you find us a way out of here.'

I nod in response to the Lieutenant's instructions. But finding a way out is proving more difficult than I thought. Taking some deep breaths, I try to calm down, and try to remember all that I can about portcullises. Perhaps I'm overlooking something.

Portcullises are defensive features, raised by a chain attached to a winch mechanism. When the winch is wound, the metal gate is lifted into the roof. Meaning this port-cullis must be able to ascend into the tunnel roof.

Surely the person who designed this passage did not intend for people escaping from the castle to get trapped down here. That is, of course, unless they had some twisted sense of humour. If that's the case, I'm sure they're laughing in their grave right now.

A terrible thought enters my mind and sends a cold shudder crawling across my skin. Slowly, I reach up to check if there's a gap in the stone above the portcullis. My heart sinks as my fingertips push into hard stone.

The portcullis was never intended to be raised. It appears to be fixed to the stone roof of the tunnel. This tunnel isn't an escape passage – it's a *death trap!*

I swallow back the wave of fear rising in my stomach and shake my head in bewilderment. This can't be right. Why bother creating this tunnel if it only leads to a fixed metal gate? A dead end? That makes no sense. Again, a voice in the back of my mind tells me that I'm overlooking something staring me straight in the face. But what?

I hear my companions priming their pistols and preparing themselves for the inevitable fight. I have to remain focused – to search for a solution to our predicament. I grip the portcullis and close my eyes in deep thought, willing it to reveal its secret. Armand's whispered warning makes me snap my head around and stare back down the tunnel, where – by the light cast by their lanterns – I see Marquis de Beynac's men stalking stealthily along the passage, no more than *thirty yards* away. Their drawn blades glisten red in the wan light – a frightening premonition of the blood they will shortly spill.

'*Get down!*' Blodklutt whispers harshly. 'Pistols first. Select your target. Make your shot count. But wait for my order.'

I know the Lieutenant instructed me to find a way out of the tunnel, but I'm not turning my back on this fight. Dropping down beside von Frankenthal, I ready my flintlock pistol – which is not an easy task in the complete darkness – and draw back the firing pin. I do this slowly, for I dare not risk making any sound that will betray our position. Then I level my firearm at the advancing soldiers and select a target.

I very much doubt the Marquis de Beynac would risk his life in entering the tunnel. I'm sure he's back in the courtyard, pulling the strings from a distance, never in personal danger. But some sixth sense tells me that Horst von Skullschnegger has come down after us. I can feel his formidable presence, almost as if his eyes are prying through the darkness into my very soul.

But which one is he? He wouldn't be the one at the front left – the balding man with the bulbous nose. I don't think it would be the man directly behind him, either. He has the anxious stance of a man who's used to receiving orders, rather than issuing them.

It could be that tall one in the middle, crouching lower than the others so as to not hit his head on the roof. He has a stocky neck and a terrific scowl that could put the fear of God into many a hardened soldier. But, again, he lacks a leader's presence of authority. Which makes me think it can't be this man after all. I imagine Horst von Skullsch-negger would combine fighting prowess and intelligence – like that man at the *rear* of the troop, clad in a royal blue doublet. Dual rapiers jostle by his thighs, and he has pene-trating eyes that warrant respect. His every move seems to bespeak confidence.

That must be Horst von Skullschnegger. And so, with the target identified, I level my pistol at his chest.

We are outnumbered, trapped, wounded and exhausted. The odds are stacked heavily against us. But we do have one thing to our advantage – the one thing that could turn the tide in our favour: the element of surprise.

Hidden in darkness as we are, the Marquis de Beynac's men cannot see us. They don't know we are lying in wait for them, monitoring their every move, our targets already selected. If we do this right, we have the chance of taking out nearly half their number before they even realise they're under attack. And so we wait, in the dark, fingers poised on triggers, watching the Marquis's men draw closer.

'Now.' Blodklutt whispers the command so softly I barely hear the order.

At that instant – with our would-be attackers barely twenty yards away – we fire. The report of our pistols, magnified in the confined space of the tunnel, is *deafening*, forcing me to turn my head away and shut my eyes tight in a vain attempt to muffle the sound.

I hear panic and confusion descend upon the Marquis's troop. There's a desperate scream, as if someone is in their death throes, and an unholy chorus of cursing and swearing. Then there's the sound of rapid retreat, and the odd, desperate pistol shot, fired with the precision of an arthritis-inflicted novice musketeer who's facing a cavalry charge and only being stopped from fleeing the battlefield by his sergeant's pistol.

Like I said, desperate shots, no harm to anybody.

That is, of course, until the hat is shot clear from my head. That was close. *Too close*. An inch lower and my brains would have been plastered over the tunnel wall.

I try shuffling back, deeper into the darkness of the tunnel, and only when I have moved back a yard or two do I look back at the Marquis's men. They have fled from the tunnel, leaving behind the lantern and three dead.

Three dead – that's a good start. We've evened the odds somewhat. But now they know we're down here, lying in wait for them, I doubt they'll make the same mistake again. And I can't see Horst von Skullschnegger amongst the dead. He must be back up in the chapel, plotting with the Marquis de Beynac, devising some other way of coming down to get us. Come after us he will, for we've just killed three of his troops. He won't stop now until he's quenched his thirst for revenge with our blood.

CHAPTER THIRTY-THREE

Minutes pass slowly, and it's deathly quiet. The abandoned lantern has lit the corridor in a wan orange light, spilling all the way back to the stairs. But we're safe, located just on the edge of its perimeter, blanketed in darkness, hidden in shadow. This is another factor to our advantage. For although we can't be seen, we'll be able to open fire on the Marquis's men the instant they descend the stairs.

Lieutenant Blodklutt finally relaxes his guard, gives the command to reload, and I turn back to the portcullis. It's at that moment, as I'm rummaging through the dark, trying to find my hat, that I discover something that makes my heart skip a beat with excitement. For my fingers have discovered a narrow crevice, no wider than an inch, and running the width of the tunnel. And it's directly *beneath* the portcullis.

The portcullis is not fixed into the stone, as I had previously thought. Rather than being raised, this portcullis must descend into the ground.

Leaping to my feet with newfound hope, I grip the iron bars. Instead of pushing upwards, I pull *downwards*. There's a grinding sound, like a coil of rusted springs being pushed tight. And the portcullis descends a good foot into the ground!

I'd take my hat off to the engineer who invented this simple ploy – that is, of course, if I could find my hat. The original inhabitants of this castle, having fled into the tunnel and escaped through the portcullis, would have found their way out of the secret passage and off into the hills whilst their pursuers would have been stuck at this barrier. A ruse so simple, yet guaranteed to perplex any pursuer, granting you enough time to escape from the tunnel and disappear into the neighboring countryside.

'We're through,' I whisper back to my companions, grinning triumphantly. 'We can get out.'

But they're not sharing my enthusiasm. For their focus is on the powder keg – with a *hissing fuse!* – that has just been rolled down the stairs and is coming down the tunnel, directly towards us!

There's a desperate scramble as my companions leap to their feet.

'Get out!' Lieutenant Blodklutt yells, his horror-filled eyes locked on the powder keg as he drags and pushes everyone back to the portcullis.

I push down on the iron barrier with all my might, lowering it a good three feet. But I don't know how long I'll be able to hold it. There is definitely a spring mechanism forcing the portcullis back up. I'm already struggling to keep it in place. A few seconds more and I fear I'll be pinned against the roof.

'Go! Get through,' I roar. 'I can't hold this much longer!'

My companions don't need any urging. Within a heartbeat they've climbed over the barrier and are making their way through the darkness, moving deeper into the tunnel. Which means that, in the panicked confusion, I've been left by myself to try to clamber over the portcullis without any assistance!

I snap my head back up the tunnel, to where the powder keg has stopped, trapped in the legs of one of the slain soldiers. It is no more than *fifteen yards* away, and the fuse is impossibly small.

My eyes wide with terror, I push down on the portcullis with all of my remaining strength. I manage to hoist over my right leg. But at that very moment I feel the barrier rise, and two pointed metal bars press hard into me. I try lifting my left foot over, but again the portcullis shifts, this time rising several feet, lifting me off the ground, and pushing my back against the roof. Don't tell me this is the way I'm going to die – impaled by a two-hundred pound metal barrier!

Feeling my strength wane, I pay a hurried glance at the powder keg, only to find that I can no longer see the fuse. It's worked its way down into the barrel. I squeeze my eyes shut in preparation for the explosion.

Suddenly I feel a powerful force push down on the port-cullis, lowering it two feet. An iron-like grip seizes me by the shirt, lifts me off the barrier, and plants me on the other side of the tunnel where there's a slim hope of life.

'You didn't think we'd leave you behind, did you? Now run!'

I'd recognise that avalanche of a voice anywhere. But von Frankenthal hardly needed to waste his breath telling me that, for I'm racing along the tunnel the second my feet touch the ground. My hands are outstretched before me, feeling my way through the darkness. I'm aware of von Frankenthal's massive frame by my side, pushing me forward, knowing that we only have seconds before . . .

KABOOM!

There's a massive explosion from behind! It rips through the tunnel, consuming everything in a blast of hot fury. Not even a heartbeat passes before it engulfs us in a storm of rubble, fire and smoke. Von Frankenthal grabs me, tries to shelter me from the impact, but we are thrown off our feet and crash heavily to the floor.

I bury my head in my hands and do all that I can under these circumstances – send a hasty prayer to survive this Hell's inferno.

An eternity seems to pass before I open my eyes. Spitting dirt from my mouth, I push myself up onto an elbow. I shake my head in disbelief, trying to come to terms with the fact that I somehow managed to survive the explosion. Then I inspect my surroundings.

It's pitch black, and as silent as a grave. Smoke and the smell of gunpowder hang heavily in the air, forcing me to cough and breathe through my sleeve. A sharp twang of pain draws my attention to a nasty gash on my left forearm. I feel the hot trickle of blood run down my hand. At least it's not life threatening. A few bandages will take care of it.

Von Frankenthal stirs by my side.

'We made it. Can you believe it?' I say, barely able to hear my own voice over my ringing ears.

Von Frankenthal coughs, clears his throat, and dusts himself off. 'I thought we were dead,' he says, his voice raised, his hearing also evidently affected by the explosion. 'It's nothing short of a miracle we survived that. Are you hurt?'

I shake my head, and try to the best of my ability to bandage the cut on my left forearm with a strip of cloth torn from my tabard. 'Nothing that a few days of rest won't heal. Yourself?'

'As bruised and battered as Hell. But I'll live. I wonder if the others were as lucky.'

It's hardly surprising that von Frankenthal should survive the blast. Like a medieval stronghold, he was built to last.

I can't understand, however, why the Marquis de Beynac sent an ignited powder keg down into the tunnel. That the tunnel roof didn't collapse is nothing short of a miracle. And if it had, how then would have the Marquis been able to locate our bodies to recover the trumpet he must assume is in our possession? Not exactly the brightest idea he could have come up with. But desperate times call for desperate measures, and he must have feared that we were going to escape with the trumpet. He must have reasoned that it was better to kill us and risk burying the Scourge of Jericho under several tonnes of stone, rather than risk having the relic remain in our possession.

Again, I find myself wondering how von Frankenthal and I managed to survive the explosion. My ears are still ringing – as I imagine they will be for some time. That was the biggest explosion I've ever seen. I imagine that a powder keg detonated out in the open would wreak a lot of damage. But to experience one being detonated within the confines of a tunnel, where its destructive power is magnified tenfold, is like having a volcano erupt under you. I can't believe it didn't bring down the passage.

It looks as if I've spoken too soon. For no sooner have I had that thought than we hear it – a low rumble, coming from back down the tunnel. The sound of *hundreds of tonnes* of stone loosened by the explosion. Ready to collapse at any moment.

'That can't be good,' I warn.

But von Frankenthal doesn't even hear me. He clambers to his feet, dragging me up after him. Then we are racing for our lives again, hurtling blindly down the tunnel, trying to put as much distance between ourselves and the area of the tunnel damaged by the explosion.

We have barely covered a few yards before we hear a heavy crash from behind. It sounds as if the entire tunnel roof has collapsed where the immediate explosion took place. But then – to my horror – I hear the low rumble start again. Only this time, it's spreading *outwards* from the area of the initial collapse. The roof of the tunnel starts to cave in, dropping massive chunks of bone-shattering stone, in a line heading straight towards us!

We race through the dark with all the speed we can muster, careening off each other into the tunnel walls. Our laboured breath wheezes through our lungs, and von Frankenthal is cursing so much he'd better hope that Heaven is turning a deaf ear. And then there's the terrifying crash of stone following from behind, getting closer with each passing second.

It's impossible to tell how far we race through the darkness, but we must have at least covered fifty yards before we hear panicked voices up ahead. A few more strides and we reach our companions, only to find them trapped at the end of the tunnel – their escape blocked by what feels to be a heavy, iron-ribbed wooden door.

'It looks like our race is run,' Armand says, struggling against the lock with what I can only assume is a dagger. 'We can't break through.'

There's no stopping von Frankenthal, however. He orders us aside, and moves back several yards, giving himself room for a run-up. Then, with a roar that rivals the sound of the collapsing roof, he charges at the door, setting his massive shoulder against it.

There's a terrific *CRUNCH*, followed instantly by the sound of splintering wood and bending metal. A blinding light fills the tunnel as the door collapses. Not missing a beat, we shield our eyes against the afternoon sun and dive out of the passage. We make it just in the nick of time. For no sooner have we exited the tunnel than the roof comes crashing down behind us – like the jaws of some giant mythological creature – engulfing us in a cloud of dust and rubble.

CHAPTER THIRTY-FOUR

I lie on my back for several minutes, staring up at the clouds, vaguely aware that I'm lying on a forested slope, somewhere beyond the perimeter of cleared ground that surrounds Schloss Kriegsberg. But all that really matters for the moment is that we survived the collapsing tunnel. Drawing back some deep breaths, I savour the fresh air, and marvel at a great irony of life – how this moment of peace can exist only a heartbeat away from the jaws of death.

'That was too close for comfort,' Armand says, stirring by my side, breaking the silence.

'You don't have to tell me that,' I say, and push myself up onto an elbow, wincing with the effort. 'Talk about scaring the life out of me. I feel as though I've aged fifty years.'

Armand smirks. 'Well, my dear lad, you're lucky there's no mirror handy.'

'Believe me – you're in no position to talk,' I return.

I can't believe the state we're in. You'd hardly suspect we are members of an elite Catholic military order. We look more like a procession of destitute street urchins who have escaped from a torture chamber. There's barely an inch of our clothing not torn or caked in blood and dirt.

'Let's leave the banter for later,' Blodklutt says, dusting himself off. He starts to reload his pistol; a sombre reminder that we aren't safe just yet. 'We've still got to get out of these mountains. With any luck, the Marquis de Beynac will think we never made it out of there alive. Let's make sure he believes that's the case. We'll make for the horses and disappear from these cursed mountains forever.'

'I'm all for that,' von Frankenthal says.

Lieutenant Blodklutt offers me a hand and hoists me to my feet. 'Then let's get out of here. Robert – you lead. Christian – you'll bring up the rear. And keep your wits about you. The Marquis de Beynac may have men patrolling the perimeter of the castle.'

We descend into the woods, but I can't help glancing over my shoulder at Schloss Kriegsberg, its walls and towers visible through breaks in the trees. Abandon all hope, ye who enter here – that was the inscription scrawled on the gatehouse portcullis; words which are now etched in my mind. It was a warning that should not have been taken lightly, for this is a place where only devils dare to tread. How we ever managed to survive the horrors of the castle I'll never know. The mission was my baptism by fire. I was thrown headfirst into the crucible of combat. Not only did it test my ability with a sword and pistol, but also my resolve, loyalties, and values I hold dear to my heart. Fortunately, I have been able to emerge from the castle without having compromised any of those values.

I've taken my first few dangerous steps into the world of a witch hunter. As dangerous as this job is, however, I know I have performed deeds of great good today. I have wielded my blade in the name of Christ, defending all that is sacred against Satan's forces. I truly believe that not only have I proven my worth to my companions, and earned my place within the Hexenjäger, but I have found my calling. Ever since I can remember, I have dreamed of following in the footsteps of my father and wielding a blade in epic battles. Up until one week ago, the only way I could fulfil this dream was through reading the books in my uncle's study and fantasising about what it would be like to enter battle. But now I feel as one with the spirit of my father, and I picture him as an older version of myself, grizzled and scarred by years of war, guiding his mount along a dusty trail, somewhere in the war-ravaged Low Countries over a decade ago.

Five minutes later we reach the clearing where our horses are tethered. We spare a few minutes tending our wounds, applying makeshift bandages and salves, and drinking heavily from the water-skins slung over our saddles.

Lieutenant Blodklutt then gives the command for us to mount, and after paying one final look at Schloss Kriegsberg, I guide my horse out of the clearing. Following behind my companions, and with Armand riding by my side, I steer my horse along the forest trail leading down the slope of the mountain. And so we begin the long journey back to the Hexenjäger barracks at Burg Grimmheim.

⚔CHAPTER⚔
THIRTY-FIVE

It is mid-afternoon as I make my way across the central courtyard in Burg Grimmheim. Two days have passed since our return, and I'm more than grateful for the opportunity to recuperate and recover from the mission to Schloss Kriegsberg. My shoulder is still bandaged, as it will be for several more days, my jaw sports a nasty bruise, and I'm covered in dozens of minor abrasions. But my wounds are nothing that rest won't heal. I'm just thankful to be secure within the heavy stone walls of Burg Grimmheim, alive and safe from the horrors that haunt the Harz Mountains.

I have just come out of a formal meeting with Grand Hexenjäger Wrangel. Armand and von Frankenthal are waiting for me in a colonnaded walkway on the opposite side of the courtyard, and they hasten over to me, expectant looks on their faces.

Armand, bandaged from head to toe, is barely able to contain his excitement. 'So are you going to tell us how you went? Please, Jakob, the suspense is killing us.'

'You were in there for quite some time,' von Frankenthal adds. 'It's not very often that the Grand Hexenjäger requests private meetings with the rank and file, particularly initiates. He must have had some important things to discuss with you.'

'He did,' I say, 'and it's going to take some time for it to sink in.'

Armand's eyes arch inquisitively. 'Take some time for *what* to sink in?'

'Grand Hexenjäger Wrangel told me that he's finally had time to read Lieutenant Blodklutt's report on the mission,' I explain. 'He wanted to personally commend me on the role I played. I was only selected as part of the team because, as a new initiate, I could not have been the spy he wished to flush out. Put simply, he knew that Captain Faust and Lieutenant Blodklutt would be able to put their trust in me. But he also feared, given the perilous nature of the mission, that I would not survive.'

I pause, building up the suspense, much to Armand's annoyance, who is hanging off my every word. He makes an exasperated gesture and says, 'And?'

'Not only was he surprised that I wasn't killed, but,

having read Blodklutt's report, he is amazed at the role I played in the mission,' I continue. 'According to him, an initiate has never before demonstrated such bravery and resourcefulness. He even went so far as to say that the success of the mission was largely due to me. And, in gratitude for my bravery, he has granted me special dispensation. There is going to be an induction ceremony held a week from today. I am going to be formally accepted as a witch hunter within the Hexenjäger.'

Armand extends a hand in congratulations, and von Frankenthal, barely able to control his enthusiasm, pats me so hard on the back that I'm practically knocked off my feet.

As much as I want to wear the crimson tabard and cape of the Hexenjäger, however, I am apprehensive about being inducted into the order. I had initially harboured fears that the Grand Hexenjäger had somehow learned that my letter of introduction was fake – and that was why he had requested a special meeting. Although this was not the case, I know that I was extremely lucky to have survived Schloss Kriegsberg. I have been given barely any training in the art of slaying witches. I have literally had to learn from experience. But my experience is so limited, and I fear that I might now find myself being sent on dangerous missions, and that my fellow Hexenjäger may have far higher expectations of me.

'Welcome to the order, brother-in-arms,' von Frankenthal smiles, his eyes beaming with pride.

'That's the best news I've heard all day. Well done, Jakob,' Armand says, elated. 'I suppose some sort of celebration is called for. What say you? We'll meet in my quarters for dinner?'

'That sounds good,' I say. 'I must admit, though, I still can't believe that this has happened. It's going to take some time to register.'

Von Frankenthal scratches his chin in thought. 'Actually, now that you've brought it to my attention, I've never heard of anyone rising so quickly in the ranks of the Hexenjäger. It's unprecedented. The normal timeframe for an initiate to become a proper witch hunter can range from six to twelve months.'

'Did I not say that you had found your calling?' Armand says proudly. 'After your first encounter with the witches – during which you slew *three* of their number – I knew that there was something special about you. No raw initiate has ever before demonstrated such fighting prowess – not even Captain Alejandro de la Cruz. It came as no great surprise to me to learn that your father had been a professional soldier. I also knew that your father's blood – the blood of a warrior – ran thick in your veins. Which reminds me, I have another surprise for you. So if you will, follow me.'

I bid farewell to von Frankenthal and, following after Armand, cross the courtyard. We enter a long single-storey building positioned on the southern side of the court-yard, its back adjoining the southern perimeter wall of the castle. Spanning off the central corridor of this building are some twenty or so private quarters. Armand directs me to the fifth door on the right, knocks, then ushers me inside.

There's a witch hunter sitting at a solitary desk in the far corner. He's puffing on a pipe, having a quiet moment of reflection as he looks out onto the courtyard through his drawn window.

'Dietrich Hommel, may I introduce Jakob von Drachenfels,' Armand announces. 'I don't know if you can remember, Jakob, but I told you that Dietrich had served in the Low Countries some ten years ago. Well, as chance would have it, he not only served in the same company as your father, but he was also one of his closest friends.'

'What?' I stammer, struggling to comprehend this revelation – that I have finally found the long-lost piece of the puzzle that will reveal the truth about my father.

'You will no doubt want some privacy. You have much to talk about,' Armand says, and patting me on the shoulder, exits the room.

'It is easy to see that you are your father's son,' Dietrich begins, studying my features. 'You have the same eyes, sharp and alert. But, please, take a seat. As Armand has said, we have much to discuss. I imagine you will have many questions.'

I pull up a seat opposite Dietrich, speechless. I have been searching for clues about my father for my entire life. But all I've ever been able to find are mere snippets of information, elusive fragments from a larger picture – a picture which, to this day, has managed to remain hidden.

I shake my head, struggling to comprehend that this is actually happening. 'I have many questions – so many, in fact, that I don't know where to begin.'

Dietrich smiles softly. 'Then let us start from the beginning, from when I first met Tobias – your father – in Aachen. It was a long time ago – over twenty years ago, in fact. Despite that, I can clearly recall the first time I ever set eyes on him. Although he was only one of several hundred soldiers who had assembled in the town square to volunteer their swords to suppress a Protestant uprising in Thuringia, he stood out from the crowd. He wasn't an officer at the time, but he had a commanding presence. He was a man of few words, but when he spoke, people listened. And it was during the suppression of that uprising that your father and I forged a friendship that would last for almost a decade.'

'I know that he was a cavalry commander in the Low Countries,' I say, eager to learn as much as I can. 'But what did he do before that? Do you know anything of his past – anything of his life before you met him in Aachen? Do you know, for instance, how he met my mother?'

Dietrich smiles and raises a hand, signalling for me to slow down. 'There's no rush. We have as long as you need.'

'I'm sorry. It's just that I've waited so long to learn these things.'

'And I will tell you all that I can. But let's just slow things down a little, shall we?' Dietrich says, his eyes becoming distant, his thoughts drifting back to events over two decades ago. He takes a long draw of his pipe before proceeding. 'It is fortunate for you that Tobias told me much about his past. I remember him telling me that he had travelled to England and fought as a mercenary for the Royalist forces during the English Civil War. During this campaign, serving in one of Prince Maurice's regiments of horse, he learned the cavalry tactics that he would later employ as a commander of horse in the Low Countries. But it wasn't until Tobias returned to the German states that he met Sophie – who would later become your mother – in his childhood town of Bremen.'

'Bremen?' I say, my eyebrows arched in curiosity. 'I never knew that.'

'He lived there until the age of fifteen, if I remember correctly.'

'And why did he leave?'

'Tobias once told me that he left home at such a young age in order to see the world, and to seek fame and glory in the army,' Dietrich explains. 'But back to Bremen – after a brief attempt at hanging up his sword he returned to the life of a professional soldier. It was during this time that I met your father in Aachen. Having become as close as brothers, we ventured into Spain as swords for hire, and found work in Castile in the service of the Count of Seville. Tobias was always torn between the instinctive call of a soldier and his love for Sophie, though. He returned to Bremen and tried to settle down. He and Sophie were married, and you were born.'

'And you actually met my mother?' I ask.

Dietrich smiles fondly. 'Yes, although only briefly. Although I wasn't present at the time of your parents' wedding – for I was still serving in Castile – I came to visit your father shortly after your birth. Sophie was a kind and gentle woman, and she loved you dearly.' He pauses as he takes another puff of his pipe. 'Having stayed with your parents for a few weeks, I returned to Castile. But family life did not agree with Tobias. He became restless, finding domestic life too quiet. Finally, unable to suppress the call of the warrior, he returned to join me in Castile, where we were awarded commissions as officers of horse. He then spent the remaining years of his life fighting alongside me in the Spanish Netherlands against the French, who we were at war with at the time, until he was killed in a skirmish at Breda – or, at least, it was *assumed* that he had been killed.'

'Assumed?' I ask, leaning forward in my seat, looking at Dietrich askance. 'What do you mean? Is there a chance that my father is still alive?'

Dietrich shrugs uncertainly. 'I don't know. Nobody

knows, in fact. He had been performing a rearguard action, commanding a troop of dragoons defending a bridge leading into the town. Although his troop had been overwhelmed by superior French numbers, he refused to abandon his position. The last I ever saw of him, he was standing in the middle of the bridge, bloodied and wounded, preparing to face a cavalry charge by the enemy's advance vanguard. It was a suicidal last stand, and as none of the dragoons returned to a designated rendezvous point later that day, it was assumed that the entire company – including Tobias – had died on the bridge.'

I study Dietrich's face intently. 'But you never actually saw my father fall, did you?'

Dietrich shakes his head. 'No. But I was consumed by a desire to discover what fate had befallen Tobias, and returned to the site of the skirmish the following day, before the dead had been buried. I could not find his body, however, and could only assume that he had been killed and fallen into the river. If he had survived, then surely he would have returned to his command, to the soldiers he considered his brothers-in-arms. But in the weeks that passed I learned that a handful of dragoons had survived the skirmish, only to be taken captive and transported deep into Dutch territory, where they were sent to rot in the rat-infested prisons of Rotterdam. These were being run by a former Dutch commander, who held a deep grudge against the Spanish and their German mercenary allies, having fought alongside the French for many years in the Low Countries, during which time the commander had lost an eye to a German musket. To be sent to these prisons was to suffer a fate worse than death.'

My heart fills with hope. 'So there is a possibility, albeit very slim, that my father is still alive – that he was not killed during the skirmish at Breda,' I say.

Dietrich gives me a glum look, as if to caution me that I should not get my hopes too high. 'The fact that Tobias has not been seen since that day can only mean that, even if he did manage to survive the skirmish, he was taken captive.'

'And so for the past twelve years he may have been shackled to some prison wall in Rotterdam.'

'It's possible,' Dietrich says. 'But from what I've heard, you are lucky if you can survive a month or two in Rotterdam's infamous gaols, let alone *twelve years*.'

But I hardly hear Dietrich's last few words. Looking through the window, I picture my father, scarred from years of fighting in the Spanish Netherlands, lying manacled in some gaol. And I know that I will not rest until I can discover the truth of what happened to my father on the bridge at Breda. I may have joined the Hexenjäger, and I intend to remain with this order for as long as I have the strength in my arms to wield a blade. But I make a solemn pledge that I will discover the truth of what happened at Breda, even if it means venturing into the Low Countries and breaking into the dankest, darkest gaols of Rotterdam.

At length, Dietrich and I resume our discussion, and for the next three hours I listen intently to all that he tells me concerning my father. The sun is setting by the time we finish. Through the window in Dietrich's quarters I notice that heavy shadows have lengthened across the courtyard, and the windows on the opposite side of the castle are illuminated by the soft glow of candlelight.

I'm amazed at how quickly the time has passed. But I have learned things this afternoon that had remained hidden for over a decade. Dietrich has blown the dust off the mystery concerning my father's identity and life. For the first time in my life, I feel complete. My father is no longer a hazy figure, an elusive ghost, for he has now taken solid form – been given flesh and blood by Dietrich's information.

'I cannot thank you enough for what you have told me,' I say, extending a hand in gratitude. 'And I'm sorry to have taken so much of your time. I didn't realise it was so late.'

'Please, do not apologise,' Dietrich says. 'It was nice to wander down the misty trails of the past, reminiscing about the times I shared with Tobias. Should you ever wish to talk of your father again, I will be more than willing to sit down with you.'

Having thanked Dietrich again, I leave his quarters. I make my way over to the mess hall, eager for some dinner, my mind distant, pondering over all that I have just learned. It's only when I am halfway across the central courtyard I remember that Armand had invited me to his quarters for dinner to celebrate my forthcoming induction as a witch hunter.

I climb a flight of stairs that leads to the eastern wing of the fortress. A dozen or so doors span off this corridor, each giving access to a witch hunter's private quarters, and I stop outside the door leading into Armand's room. Hearing voices from within, I knock before entering, to find that Armand, von Frankenthal, Lieutenant Blodklutt, Robert and – much to my surprise – Sabina, my friend from the kitchen, have gathered in the room.

Armand greets me and ushers me into his quarters. 'What kept you so long? I was beginning to wonder if you had forgotten about our little celebration.'

'I almost did,' I confess, noting that some trays of food and a casket of claret are positioned atop a desk in a corner of the room, the walls of which are adorned with Armand's private collection of over a dozen swords. 'I lost track of time talking with Dietrich.'

'I hope it all went well?' Robert asks.

'I've learned a lot about my father,' I say, nodding. 'But yes, it all went well.'

I am about to inform my friends that there is a slim possibility that my father might still be alive, albeit locked in the gaols of Rotterdam, when Armand pats me on the shoulder and asks the other Hexenjäger to draw their blades in my honour. As Sabina withdraws to a corner of the room, a proud smile on her lips, the witch hunters draw their swords, form a circle, and cross their blades in a symbolic union of brotherhood.

'To Jakob,' Armand says. '*Deo duce, ferro comitante.*'

'To Jakob!' the witch hunters say, then repeat the creed of the Hexenjäger.

'Congratulations, Jakob,' Armand says as he sheathes his blade, his eyes beaming with pride, almost as if I were his younger brother. 'It won't be long and you will soon be wearing the crimson tabard and cape of a fully fledged Hexenjäger. Your efforts in Schloss Kriegsberg have not gone unrewarded.'

I look down in modesty. 'A lot of it was luck.'

Lieutenant Blodklutt considers me with his impassive steel-grey eyes. 'I know. And you should not forget that,' he says, making my eyes snap back up, surprised by the brusqueness of his comment. 'Don't forget that it takes years to learn the art of slaying Satan's servants. Do not let this appointment give you a false sense of confidence. You still have much to learn.'

Shaking her head, Sabina comes over, hooks an arm under mine in a protective manner, and shoots the Lieutenant a reprimanding look. 'You all have much to learn, especially you, Blodklutt, particularly in the art of learning how to relax. And would it hurt to allow Jakob to have a few moments to bask in the glory of his upcoming induction ceremony?' She then looks at me. 'The poor Lieutenant doesn't know that he's allowed to come off duty. I'm sure

Blodklutt sleeps with one eye open and with a hand on his rapier.'

I look apologetically at Lieutenant Blodklutt, embarrassed that Sabina – a kitchen-hand, free from the formalities of rank that govern the relationships of the Hexenjäger – has placed me in this situation. Despite the reprimand, however, the Lieutenant cannot help but smile, and pats me on the shoulder in a rare token of affection. He then wanders around the room, inspecting Armand's collection of swords.

'You're brave,' von Frankenthal says, looking at Sabina.

'I was merely speaking the truth,' she says, somewhat defensively.

Armand grins, observing the way in which Sabina has hooked her arm under mine. 'Wild horses could not have kept her away from this private celebration,' he tells me, receiving a glare from Sabina. 'When I went down to the kitchen to collect some food and drink for this evening, and she overheard that I was hosting a small celebration for you, she practically pinned me against the wall, wanting to know what it was all about.'

'Oh, do be quiet,' Sabina scolds and takes a step away from me, suddenly conscious of the way in which she had been holding my arm. 'I did no such thing.'

'Behave yourself, Armand,' von Frankenthal says, suppressing a grin and trying to put on a stern expression. 'Leave the girl alone. Besides, should not Sabina have been the first person to be invited? It is, when all is said and done, a celebration in honour of her *significant other*.'

Sabina's eyes go wide with embarrassment, and her foot lashes out, kicking the witch hunter in the shin. 'Hold your tongue, you great oaf!' she says, pointing a finger at von Frankenthal in warning. 'Or my next kick won't be directed at your shin. And don't you dare say that Jakob is my suitor, for he is not.'

'Leave her alone,' I say, finding it impossible not to laugh at von Frankenthal as he rubs his shin in pain. 'Or I will be forced to defend her, Revelation 6.8.'

Hearing me call him that, von Frankenthal shoots Armand a reproachful look. The Frenchman holds up his hands in a defensive manner, and puts on a shocked expression so as to suggest that he had nothing to do with me learning the nickname.

'I swear to God, I have no idea how he learned that,' he says. 'All I can think is that Jakob must have worked it out for himself. There is, after all, a striking similarity between you and the fourth rider of the Apocalypse.'

I'm laughing so hard that I don't even notice von Frankenthal cuff me playfully over the head.

Observing all of this from a corner of the room, Lieutenant Blodklutt rolls his eyes. 'I have a feeling this is going to be a long evening.'

Historical notes

The Witch Hunter Chronicles is a mix of historical fact and the workings of my fertile imagination. Whilst I have taken care to ensure the world is authentic, I have certainly taken liberties with some of the events and military units presented in *The Scourge of Jericho*. No doubt there will be some readers who want to know more about the world of The Witch Hunter Chronicles, so I have included this section to provide more information on the novel's setting, weaponry and military organisations. By no means is this intended to provide a complete history of the seventeenth century, but it will at least answer some of your questions, and hopefully whet your appetite, inspiring you to research more into what I consider to be the most fascinating period in history.

HISTORICAL SETTING

Seventeenth-century Germany was very different to the country we know today. The country, in fact, was not even known as 'Germany', but comprised several hundred independent states, principalities and cities, the borders of which were constantly changing. Referred to as the 'German states' or the 'German-speaking lands', these territories were part of the larger Holy Roman Empire. With its capital set in Vienna, and ruled by the Habsburg Holy Roman Emperor, this was a vast and cosmopolitan empire, stretching from Hungary in the east to the Netherlands in the west, and from the North Sea to parts of present-day Italy.

During the period in which The Witch Hunter Chronicles takes place, the boundaries of the Holy Roman Empire had been established by the Treaty of Westphalia of 1648. This treaty, which effectively brought an end to the Thirty Years' War, saw the Holy Roman Empire lose much territory and power. Of particular importance to The Witch Hunter Chronicles, this treaty saw the Netherlands gain independence from the Holy Roman Empire, resulting in the creation of the Dutch Republic. Jakob's father was one of thousands of German soldiers who fought alongside the Spanish against the French in the Netherlands.

ORDERS AND MILITARY UNITS

The Hexenjäger: Is the German term for witch hunters, who were operating in every state of Germany during the seventeenth century. These members of the Catholic and Protestant Churches were responsible for sending thousands of innocent people to be burned alive at the stake. Much to many readers' dismay, there was no specific unit called the 'Hexenjäger'; this is purely a product of my imagination. Sadly, Burg Grimmheim and the members of the Order – yes, Jakob and Armand, too – were also given birth in the misty realm of my imagination.

However, some witch hunters mentioned in the novel did exist. Johann Georg Fuchs von Dornheim, the Witch Bishop of Bamberg, was active in Franconia in the 1620s, sending hundreds of accused witches to their deaths. Many of his victims had been subjected to torture in his dreaded witch-prison – the Drudenhaus – the walls of which were covered with pages from the Bible. His son, the tattoo-covered Heinrich von Dornheim, is fictitious.

The Witch Finder General Matthew Hopkins, likewise, existed. Arguably England's most famous witch hunter, he was particularly active in East Anglia during the period of the English Civil War. The account of him hunting witches across the Yorkshire Dales is a product of my imagination.

The Brotherhood of the Cross: This unit and its members are purely fictitious.

The Grey Musketeers: The King's Musketeers, immortalised by the works of Alexandre Dumas, were an elite unit of the King of France's household guard. Regarded as one of France's finest fighting forces, the musketeers were renowned for their martial prowess, having a reputation for acts of foolhardy valour.

I'm sure some readers will be intrigued to know that Charles de Batz-Castelmore (better known as D'Artagnan) was a real-life commander of one of the musketeer companies. Although he hasn't been written into *The Scourge of Jericho*, he is one of my favourite historical personalities and will most *definitely* appear in later books.

The King's Secret: This organisation actually existed, but in the eighteenth century. It was a unit of spies controlled by the King of France. Not even the French government knew of its existence.

The Knights Templar: A military organisation of monks formed in Jerusalem during the period of the Crusades. What had started as a knightly order governed by strict vows of abject poverty, however, accrued immense wealth and developed into an extremely powerful political and military organisation. Philip the Fair, King of France, envious of the wealth and power of the Knights Templar, orchestrated their downfall and accused the order of devil worship. And so it was, in the early fourteenth century, that the Templars, branded as heretics, were tortured and burned to death in their thousands. Even the grand master of the Templars, Jacques de Molay, was burned alive, and in 1312 the order was dissolved.

The political structure of the Hexenjäger is modelled on that of the Knights Templar.

The Inquisition: An institution created by the Roman Catholic Church to eradicate all forms of heresy.

Louis XIV's Royal Palace Cavalry: This unit, as far as I know, is fictitious. Armand, a former Captain of this prestigious unit, is based on the cavalier swordsmen who sauntered into Paris searching for employment in the military organisations of the day. The most daring of these were often from Gascony, a region of France famous for its haughty, devil-may-care swordsmen. As an interesting note, Charles de Batz-Castelmore (D'Artagnan) was a Gascon.

WEAPONS AND DUELS

Swords: The primary weapon favoured by the Hexenjäger is a rapier. The use of these long-bladed duelling swords became less common by the late seventeenth century, as changes in fashion impeded their effective use. The German town of Solingen was famous for the quality of its blades.

Jakob uses a Pappenheimer rapier, a type of blade named after Count Gottfried Heinrich Graf von Pappenheim, one of the most daring cavalry officers fighting on the side of the Catholic League during the Thirty Years' War. Fierce and reckless in combat, he was shot in the lung at the Battle of Lutzen in 1632. Lying in the back of a wagon, choking on blood, he refused to die until he had confirmation that the commander of the enemy forces, the Swedish King, Gustavus Adolphus, the Lion of the North, had been killed.

Sabres, such as those wielded by Armand, were commonly used in the time of The Witch Hunter Chronicles. Heavier than rapiers, these robust, curved-blade broadswords were often used by cavalry, the combined impetus of the charging horse and swinging blade delivering a devastating blow.

Firearms: Contrary to popular belief, rifles existed in the seventeenth century. There are reports of them being used by hunters and gamekeepers in the English Civil War, which predates The Witch Hunter Chronicles by some twenty years. These firearms had rifled barrels – meaning that they had a spiralling groove on the inside of the barrel – which gave the ball (bullets didn't exist back in those days) far greater distance and accuracy.

The pistols and carbines used by the Hexenjäger are equipped with a flintlock firing mechanism. This was much more effective than the contemporary matchlock pistols and carbines, which used a lit length of cord to ignite the powder pan, and for this reason tended to malfunction when it rained. A further advantage of the flintlock pistol was that it could be preloaded; the firing pin, or cock, could be pulled back into a half-locked position. This allows Jakob to have his pistols tucked into his belt, ready to blast at the first witch to rear its head.

Grenades: Grenades existed back in the seventeenth century. They were essentially hollow cannonballs filled with gunpowder and ignited by a lit fuse. For dramatic effect, the damage dealt by the grenade used by Kurt von Wolfenbüttel has been exaggerated. The reference to the grenade being used at Hampstead Bridge is fictitious.

Duels: I have taken some liberties here. The Witch Hunter Chronicles depicts Europe, in particular the French capital, as besieged by duellists who draw their swords at the slightest provocation, every street corner being host to some matter of honour that could only be satisfied through drawn steel. Whilst this had certainly been the case in the early seventeenth century, edicts passed by the French monarchs had outlawed duels in France long before the 1660s. It was more than likely that duels still occurred in the French capital, but not to the extent that I present.

WITCHES

Witchcraft: The seventeenth century was a period in which people believed in the Devil and witchcraft. Tens of thousands of heretics (people who did not follow, or criticised, the doctrines of the Roman Catholic Church) were condemned to death as witches. These victims of the Inquisition came from all sectors of society.

The Blood Countess: Although Countess Gretchen Kraus is fictitious, she is based on the real-life Transylvanian Countess, Elizabeth Báthory, who bathed in the blood of maidens in an attempt to avoid ageing. Interestingly, Bram Stoker, the author of *Dracula*, modelled Count Dracula off Elizabeth Báthory and Vlad Tepes. Vlad Tepes was a Transylvanian Prince who defended the easternmost territories of the Holy Roman Empire against the armies of Islam, often performing acts of extreme cruelty, of which impalement was his preferred method of execution.

Walpurgis Night: Back in the seventeenth century, it was commonly believed that on the night of April 30 – when a pagan festival would be held to celebrate the last day of winter – witches performed Sabbaths (black masses). The Harz Mountains of central Germany have a long history of witchcraft, particularly Brocken Mountain. Schloss Kriegsberg, however, is a product of my imagination.

Grimoires: These are evil texts that are used to summon demons. The most famous of these texts is the *Clavis Salomonis*, the Key of Solomon, created during the Middle Ages.

Malleus Maleficarum: Arguably the most infamous book written in history, the *Malleus Maleficarum* – the Hammer of the Witches – existed. Created by the Inquisitors

James Sprenger and Heinrich Kramer, this text was used throughout the sixteenth and seventeenth centuries as the Inquisitor's handbook on how to detect witches. In The Witch Hunter Chronicles, the text is riddled with cryptic passages which, when deciphered, unlock powerful spells.

BIBLICAL RELICS

The Scourge of Jericho: As stated in the Bible, seven trumpets and the Ark of the Covenant were used by the tribes of Israel to destroy the Canaanite city of Jericho. The appearance of one of these trumpets – the Scourge of Jericho – in Württemberg is purely fictitious.

The trumpets and the Ark of the Covenant were stored for a period of time in the Temple of Solomon, which the Knights Templar happened to use as their headquarters in the Holy Land. Many people believe that they came across these treasures and used them to accrue their great wealth and power.

SELECT BIBLIOGRAPHY

Childs, John, *Warfare in the Seventeenth Century*, London, Cassell & Co., 2001

Cohen, Richard, *By the Sword: Gladiators, Musketeers, Samurai Warriors, Swashbucklers and Olympians*, New York, Pan Macmillan, 2002

Maund, Kari and Phil Nanson, *The Four Musketeers: The True Story of D'Artagnan, Porthos, Aramis and Athos*, Stroud, Tempus Books, 2005)

Summers, Montague, *The Malleus Maleficarum of Heinrich Kramer and James Sprenger*, Peter Smith Publisher, New York, 1971

Withers, Harvey J.S., *The Illustrated Encyclopedia of Swords and Sabres*, Alto Books, London, 2008

Acknowledgements

This book has come so far from when the idea of The Witch Hunter Chronicles first came to me whilst exploring the medieval town of Rothenburg ob der Tauber – which everybody must see at least once in their lifetime – to the finished product you are holding in your hands. The book has evolved so much from its initial draft: the title has changed, characters have changed – some have even changed gender! – and major plot developments have been added.

There are many people who have helped me with this book. First and foremost, I am particularly grateful to my publisher, Zoe Walton. From our initial meeting one rainy afternoon in a coffee shop in North Sydney, she has had complete faith in The Witch Hunter Chronicles. Without her belief in me, *The Scourge of Jericho* might still be sitting as an unpolished draft on a shelf in my study.

Writing can be a lonely profession. Sometimes I can spend an entire day bent over my laptop, trying to get a fight scene just right. It is during these moments that my children – my three little musketeers: Winter, Ronan and Willow – have provided me inspiration, often sitting on my lap, demanding to be read excerpts from the novel and offering their advice. Although Willow is too young to speak, her *goos* and *gaas* often guide me in the right direction.

A special thank you must be given to my editors, Cristina Briones and Abigail Nathan, for bringing the book to life, going through the manuscript with a fine-tooth comb and leaving no stone unturned. I am in gratitude to my family and friends, who have provided me invaluable encouragement and support: to my brothers, Gavin and Warren Daly; to all of my work colleagues, particularly Brian Downton and David Miller; to Lana Kaschella and to Ben Rekic, who is a never-ending source of bizarre historical information; to Joe and Lisa Gioia, Pat and Alan Birkhead, Jackie and Tony Harb, Robert and Lesley Gioia, Grace Silvio, David Lynch, Sally Beardmore, Alan and Caroline Dearn, Danielle O'Hara, Jessica Hodgson, Shayne Mikkelsen, Sharon Knight and Lea Sutherland.

None of this would have been possible without the support of my wife, Belinda. From the moment I first put pen to paper, she has encouraged me to follow my dreams and never look back.

And finally, to you, the reader. A book is only as strong as its readership. With your continued support, I hope to take the Hexenjäger on many – *many!* – more adventures.

About the Author

Stuart is a History teacher in a private high school in Sydney. Inspired by the works of Dumas, Pérez-Reverte and Matthew Reilly, and drawing upon his knowledge of the English Civil War and the Thirty Years' War, he has long considered writing an action-packed adventure series set in the seventeenth century. His biggest fan – and critic – is his six-year-old daughter, who can often be found sitting on his lap in his study as he types away on his next novel. *The Scourge of Jericho* is his first book, and he is currently working on further titles in The Witch Hunter Chronicles.

THE WITCH HUNTER CHRONICLES

BOOK TWO: THE ARMY OF THE UNDEAD

The Watchers.

Four fallen angels who have roamed the earth for several millennia, searching for the Tablet of Breaking – a device which, when activated, will destroy the world.

When the resurrected corpse of a prophet reveals that the relic lies hidden in the lost city of Sodom, Jakob and his companions, their blades still slick with the blood of slain witches, are sent to locate the Tablet before it falls into the hands of the Watchers.

Pursued by an army of undead, the mission is a desperate race against time. From the cliff-top monasteries of Meteora to a trap-riddled mausoleum lying at the bottom of the Dead Sea, the Hexenjäger must stay one step ahead of the fallen angels – for the cost of failure will mean Armageddon!

Coming soon . . .